They do things differently there

RED FOX DEFiniTiONS

Also available in **DEFiNiTiONS**

They do things differently there

Jan Mark

RED FOX DEFINITIONS

For Alison Gomm

A Red Fox Book

Published by Random House Children's Books
20 Vauxhall Bridge Road, London SW1V 2SA

A division of The Random House Group Limited
London Melbourne Sydney Auckland
Johannesburg and agencies throughout the world

First published in Great Britain by
The Bodley Head Children's Books 1994

This Red Fox edition 2001

1 3 5 7 9 10 8 6 4 2

Printed and bound in Great Britain by
Bookmarque Ltd, Croydon, Surrey

Papers used by The Random House Group are natural, recyclable products
made from wood grown in sustainable forests. The manufacturing
processes conform to the environmental regulations
of the country of origin.

The Random House Group Limited Reg. No. 9540009

www.randomhouse.co.uk

ISBN 0 09 941397 3

Contents

STALEMATE

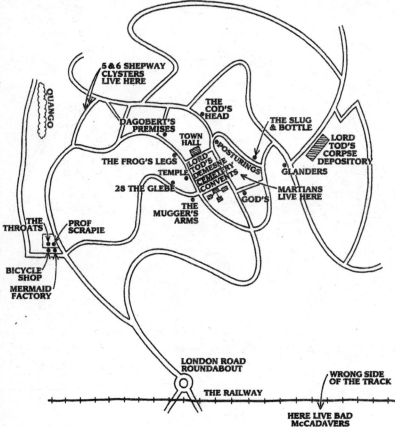

5 & 6 SHEPWAY CLYSTERS LIVE HERE

QUANGO

THE COD'S HEAD

DAGOBERT'S PREMISES

THE SLUG & BOTTLE

LORD TOD'S CORPSE DEPOSITORY

TOWN HALL

LORD TOD'S DEMESNE POSTURINGS

THE FROG'S LEGS

CEMETERY

GLANDERS

TEMPLE

CONVERTS

28 THE GLEBE

MARTIANS LIVE HERE

GOD'S

THE THROATS

PROF SCRAPIE

THE MUGGER'S ARMS

BICYCLE SHOP

MERMAID FACTORY

LONDON ROAD ROUNDABOUT

WRONG SIDE OF THE TRACK

THE RAILWAY

HERE LIVE BAD McCADAVERS

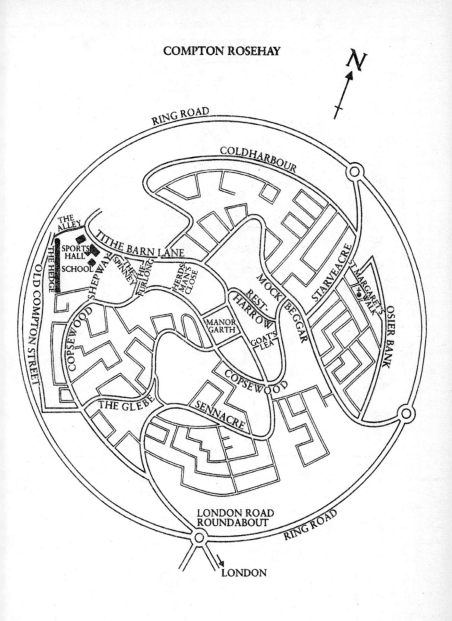

— 1 —
Creation Myth

The Martians came to Stalemate on a night of luminous calm. It was summer. A balmy haze obscured the stars, the moon was gibbous and yet to rise when a small matt-black capsule entered the ionosphere, fired its retro-rockets and descended silently, unobserved, making landfall in the flower beds outside the convent of the Combat Sisters. It was midnight; still. The seven occupants of the capsule filed out on to the lawn and stretched their forty-two cramped limbs, before stealing nimbly away into the darkness. The first that anyone in Stalemate knew of this was at 8.45 the following morning. The nuns, rising early for Prime, had observed the capsule, inadequately concealed in a ceanothus bush, but assuming it to contain a message from the Pope decided to examine it later, after Sister Orthodontia had had a chance to run the Geiger counter over it.

Mrs McCadaver, at 28 The Glebe, was washing up the breakfast dishes when she heard a discreet knock at the front door, which surprised her since there was a perfectly good set of electric tubular bells that played a muted, tasteful chime. On going to answer the door she discovered in the porch a soberly-dressed man with four arms.

'Tell me,' he said, raising his hat politely, 'have you ever had any thoughts about the after-life?'

All this happened long ago, but it was still some way in the future on the day I quarrelled with Rowena Gibbs and walked home through Old Compton for the first time. I had not meant to walk through Old Compton; the quarrel erupted unexpectedly.

'Can I borrow your *Macbeth* notes?' Rowena asked

3

as we strolled down the school drive at the end of the afternoon.

'When I've finished writing them up,' I said.

'You told me I could have them tonight.'

I was feeling surly. 'Well, it's not tonight, is it? It's this afternoon. I'll let you have them later.'

'I need them now. I'm going out later.'

'Then you'll have to do without, won't you?' I said. I wouldn't have snapped like that at anyone else, but I was tired of doing Rowena's homework.

'Selfish cow,' Rowena said.

'Or you might even try writing your own,' I suggested.

'Stuck-up bitch.' 'Snob.' 'Swot,' said our other friends loyally. As far as I could see, the insults had nothing to do with my refusing to hand over the notes before I had finished with them, but it was the spirit of the thing that counted, not accuracy.

The four of us were out in Tithe Barn Lane, now. Since we all lived in the same direction—everyone in Compton Rosehay lives in the same direction, that is part of the plot—the only way I could avoid trailing sulkily in the rear was to turn left instead of right. That took me to the end of the lane in a couple of minutes. Then I had the choice of striding purposefully down a cul-de-sac of sheltered accommodation or taking a scenic walk along the back of the sports hall. Behind me a voice called out, 'Where does she think she's going, then?'

I had to look as though I knew where I thought I was going. I turned left again, past the sports hall and mercifully out of sight of Rowena and the others, although not out of earshot.

'Only slags go round there. Who do you think wants *you*?' Marie bawled.

'Charlotte the harlot!' That was Lynzi. I hadn't

thought she'd know a word like harlot. There are much easier ones that mean the same thing.

I was on a stretch of concreted road meant for overspill parking. It led nowhere, while it was a road, but at the end of it were three bollards marking the mouth of an alley-way. The taunts of Rowena, Marie and Lynzi were still faintly audible over the roof of the sports hall; they were waiting for me to hit a dead-end, reappear sheepishly, confess my faults, hand over the *Macbeth* notes and be received back into the fold. I entered the alley.

Long ago tarmac had been laid along it, but weeds had broken through, vigorous thorn bushes met over it, only slightly above head height. It was clear that very few people ever came this way. No one with any sense would walk it after dark. Accustomed to the spacious streets of Compton Rosehay, I felt nervous about treading along a path so overgrown and unkempt and therefore possibly dangerous. Automatic security lighting had entered my soul. It was the kind of place where maniacs, perverts and molesters would hang out, I felt sure, and I was not sorry when the alley turned slightly and I saw a second trio of bollards marking the far end. I glanced once over my shoulder to make sure that no molester was on my heels, and passed between the bollards, into another world. I had left Compton Rosehay behind at the far end of the alley-way and emerged into somewhere I knew about, but had never expected to see, a place only fifteen minutes from home and five from school: Old Compton.

People who do not believe in Darwin's theory of evolution have trouble accounting for fossils. Some maintain that God created them at the same time as he created everything else and sneakily slipped them in under the bedclothes, as it were, to give people something to think about. There was a man called

Archbishop Usher who worked out that this happened at 9 a.m. on 23 October 4004 BC, everything created all at once, and while God was making fossils he knocked off Compton Rosehay and stuck it down in the middle of farm land, twenty miles out of London. This would have been around 12.30, by my calculations, when he was getting bored and starting to think about lunch.

Compton Rosehay looks as if it was made all at the same time, in a mould, and carefully disguised, like the fossils, to appear extremely old. It is quaintly faked out of mellow red brick, with terracotta tiles on the roofs, and half-timbering and ancient Tudor chimneys to let out the ancient central heating fumes; olde worlde double garages with electronic doors to house the olde worlde Rovers and Vauxhalls. The streets have phoney historical names like Coldharbour, Mockbeggar, Sennacre, Starveacre, Copsewood, The Furlong, and if there ever was a tithe barn in Tithe Barn Lane it is under the sports hall now. Even the shopping centre, which came straight out of the same mould complete with a Venetian clock tower, is called Manor Garth. There are three pubs, The Woolpack, The Drovers and The Dog and Partridge, and a wine bar, Robin Hood's. All the brickwork has diamond patterns in rows so you feel as if you are living in a petrified Fair Isle pullover.

I didn't care about any of this at first. Compton Rosehay was just a new town where we were going to live, and it was nice; a lot cleaner than the old town where we had been living, with open country all round, a new railway station only three miles away, and a link to the motorway. God created Lord John Randyll's Comprehensive School at the same time, along with half a dozen middle and first schools all named after Lord John's dim relations, and I thought Lord John's was all right—at first. It was big and clean and well-equipped (it's still big) and God created eight hundred and fifty students to fill it, and forty-three teachers. We had a house in Coldharbour with a fitted kitchen and carpets and a security light that came on automatically, and a real tree created just for us already growing in the front garden. It was all all right until I went to the library and saw the maps.

There were two of them, huge things, in frames on the wall. One was just sad. It showed what had been there before God created Compton Rosehay. Originally there were two villages, one slightly bigger than the other. The little one was called Rosehay. It was so little you could count the houses, twenty of them, scattered round a crossroads with a pub and a church and a post office. The bigger village was really just a street, with buildings straggling along it. It was called Compton. I looked at that map for a long while, thinking that these places must be quite close by and that it would be nice to visit them sometime. Then I noticed the other map.

It was a map of a town, almost perfectly circular, with a road running right round it where a junction led out on to the motorway link. In the middle was a shopping centre, Manor Garth, and leading from it, to the ring road, streets that ought to have been straight, like spokes, but had been made to curve and double back on themselves as if they were following the paths of ancient farm tracks. In between them were tucked cul-de-sacs and closes and crescents. At the bottom of the map was the name of this place, Compton Rosehay.

I looked from one map to the other until I understood. This was where I lived. Compton Rosehay, with its phoney ancient streets and its phoney ancient houses and its phoney ancient name, had been created, *whole*, and dumped down on top of those

7

two little villages. The one that had been Rosehay was right under it which accounted, I now realized, for the occasional really old house among all the fake old ones. At the side of the map, like a chord cutting across a circle, just inside the curve of the ring road, was the other village: Old Compton.

I had never located Old Compton because it was not on the way to or from any of the places I ever went to, but after discovering the maps I couldn't help noticing Rosehay. At the end of our street, Cold-harbour, there was a big Victorian house. Next time I passed it I looked at the name over the door: The Old Vicarage; so I guessed that the church must be not too far away, and went to find it. I'd have thought that a church would be hard to miss, but it was no older than the vicarage and built of red brick, so it did not stand out the way a stone one would have done, and it had no tower, just a kind of shelter on the roof at one end, with a bell hanging in it, a bell that never rang.

According to the map in the library, the pub was somewhere nearby, not one of the created pubs but the original Rosehay local. I found it in the end, half-way along Starveacre. It was called the Trafalgar Inn and the sign, with Lord Nelson on it, was still hanging outside, but it wasn't a pub any more; someone was living in it. There were wagon wheels with clematis trained through them leaning against the walls, and a row of those stone mushrooms called staddles—only these were made of concrete—along the edge of the front garden, and a huge Victorian lavatory pan with geraniums growing in it, right by the front door. I bet somebody thought that was really witty. You could imagine what the owners said to visitors when they asked where the loo was.

It took me a couple of weekends, but at last I discovered the whole of Rosehay, and by that time I was wishing that I had never started looking. I don't know who used to live in Rosehay, but they couldn't have been the people who live here now. They were probably farmers and labourers, not the people who built extensions that were bigger than the cottages they extended, and installed double garages and double glazing, drove the estate cars and four-wheel-drives that stood on the gravel forecourts, oh no. Those early inhabitants had got out fast when they looked up, one morning, and saw God lowering Compton Rosehay on top of them, like someone putting down a loaded tray without looking to see what's underneath because they can't carry it any farther.

After I found Rosehay, I didn't want to go looking for Old Compton and now, without looking for it at all, I had found it.

What had happened to Compton, when it was down-graded to *Old* Compton, was even worse than what had happened to Rosehay. The alley I had walked down sloped all the way, so that the street I was standing in now was much lower than Tithe Barn Lane. On one side lay a little patch of over-grown allotments, and at the end of them was a sheer bank that ran parallel to the street. Along the crest of it was a row of tall close conifers which I recognized as being the same tall conifer hedge that skirts our school field, only on our side is a chain link fence, four metres high. I had never once wondered what lay beyond it. Now I knew.

The straggling narrow street that was Old Compton was completely cut off by that barrier from Compton Rosehay. No doubt God had created the conifers fully grown. It was hard to imagine seeds being involved, the hedge was so hard and solid. On the other side of the street, Old Compton was hemmed in by the ring road which ran there on an embankment. All that could be seen was a grassy slope and the crash barriers along the top.

I started walking. I had no idea if I should find an exit at the far end or if I would have to retrace my steps in order to get out again. In either case I should be late home, but I doubted if my mother would worry, she would think that I was loitering with my friends along the mediaeval paths of Compton Rosehay, and Compton Rosehay is so *safe*. Anyway, I could always ring her from a call-box, if I could find one; which I was beginning to doubt. Old Compton had not so much been hemmed in as cut off, amputated. It was withering away. It could never have been a pretty village but that was hardly an excuse for what was being done to it. I passed a row of eight cottages, and five of them had very weatherbeaten FOR SALE boards outside. The post office was closed down; old notices were curling in the window and there were still three yellowed post-cards in a little glass case by a concrete square set in the pavement where the telephone box must once have stood.

More cottages, then another shop, boarded up. A chapel; a big double-fronted villa, also for sale; another chapel, then a third. None of them looked as if anyone worshipped there any longer.

There was no one about, not even cats. I saw one parked car and a motor bike standing outside a house, but no traffic passed me. The end of the street where the alley-way came out was closed off by the embankment of the ring road, but seeing the parked car made me hope that there would be a way out at the far end, unless the car had been sealed in when the village was severed. Still, it looked quite new, and then I found proof that Old Compton was not yet quite extinct. As I followed the curve of the street, which was not as straight as it had looked on the map in the library, I heard music. It was real music, a symphony, not Compton Rosehay music which God had created with one finger on an electronic keyboard. It was coming from the open door of a house on the left, one of those where the back garden ran up to the foot of the bank where the conifers stood. A privet hedge, rough and untrimmed, with bits sticking out of it which suggested that unlike a Compton Rosehay hedge it was actually *growing*, stood between the house and the street. I glanced over at the gate as I went by. It was one of those houses where the back door is in a line with the front one and I could see right through the house, into the garden beyond. I wanted to stand and stare, but I had been conditioned not to do that by three years in Compton Rosehay. In Compton Rosehay, if people see someone standing staring at their house, they ring the police.

The buildings were thinning out. I passed one last shop, the saddest of all. The lettering over the window read *The Old Forge Antiques* and I was glad it said old and not olde, but the thought of anyone trying to sell antiques in this forlorn place made my eyes fill with tears. I imagined them, day after day, hopefully opening the shop and waiting for the customers who never came, for this shop, I realized, was not derelict. The opening hours were displayed on the door and there were actually things for sale in the window; a threadbare tapestry footstool, three chamber pots, the inevitable jug and basin from a wash-stand and a leather-bound Bible, bigger than the footstool. They were not antiques, just second-hand, or third, or fourth. I felt worse than ever. What I had imagined was obviously the truth; no one would ever buy these things. The people who would once have driven through Old Compton now travelled on the motorway. The people who still lived in

Old Compton must presumably do their shopping in the Manor Garth since there were no other shops left in the village.

I must look out for them in future, they would surely be easy to identify; dusty, furtive creatures like refugees, old and hopeless, clutching worn shopping bags and baskets on wheels, dazed and intimidated in the supermarkets, humiliated in the arty boutiques of The Cloister, a bijou arcade which You-know-who had caused to exist out of reconstituted stone between Robin Hood's and the Health Centre which is not, surprisingly, called Ye House of Physick. And as this was the only route out of Old Compton, apart from the alley behind the sports hall, they must pass, every time, the antique shop.

The street was cut off again, at the far end, by the curve of the ring road whose silhouette was dominated by a great slabby blue sign announcing the presence of the motorway link and the roundabout, but a stretch of raw corrugated concrete ran uphill to the left and at the top was a bus stop where one of our newly-created mini-buses was waiting, one that would take me back along The Glebe, into the heart of Compton Rosehay, back to the land of living fossils. It was a roundabout route, but still quicker than walking and I wanted to get home. There was one other person on the bus and I could tell at once, by her clothes and her hair-style, that she could not possibly have come from Old Compton but must live in one of the town houses opposite, the row with Anglo-Saxon porches. She was Compton Rosehay through and through, created along with the town, a living fossil; like me.

I climbed on board the orange bus and paid thirty pence which, it says in the Ten Commandments, is the fare for any journey inside the ring road, and sat down as far away as possible from Fossil Woman.

Looking back down the concrete road I had just walked up, I saw the very edges of Old Compton; an empty shop with a bicycle wheel on a bracket above the door, a brick wall with ivy tossed over it like a duvet, a greenhouse with all the glass gone and, right on the boundary of Compton Rosehay, a big dirty iron shed at the end of a sloping driveway, with a broken sign that read, inappropriately, O GLEE . . . It began to rain.

I sat in the bus and waited to feel completely, desperately miserable, but there was something preventing it, something bright and cheerful fluttering in the darkness. I concentrated, and identified it; that view of the garden through the doorway of the house where human music played, a shining rectangle of hope. What had I seen? Grass, and flowering currant; a broken chair with a basket standing on it, a line of washing; I could see it still. I hardly noticed when the doors of the bus slumped shut and we began to move; I was remembering stories that I had read, where a beautiful garden is glimpsed through a door or a gate in a wall; and the person who sees it longs to enter, but something stops him, he has an appointment, he's getting married, he has to hurry on, and he can never find the door again until—

I didn't think my vision was like that, I was sure I could find it again, down the alley, behind the sports hall, beyond the conifer hedge. There was nothing magical about what I had seen, far from it. I thought of that line of washing in the garden with the flowering currant. What I had seen was Big Knickers.

— 2 —
Big Knickers

My mother loved everything about Compton Rosehay, except our next-door neighbours. When we first moved into 236 Coldharbour there were some Very Nice People living at 238. Compton Rosehay is full of VNPs. When you look into their ears you can see daylight on the other side. Unfortunately, our VNPs had left, a few months before, and the Cattermoles had moved in.

Mr Cattermole was all right, Very Nice, in fact. He got into his car every morning and drove to the railway station where he got a train to London. This was proper. This was the first of the the Ten Commandments: Thou shalt commute to work. Mrs Cattermole also had a job, part-time at the Health Centre, and that too was part of canon law: Woman was created to work part-time. The problem was Mrs Cattermole's washing line and, worst of all, what Mrs Cattermole hung on it.

The Compton Rosehay washing line was created in the form of a spider's web on a pole, and when not in use it is folded up like an umbrella. Some people even have tubular plastic cosies to slip over the top, to keep the rain off when they are folded up; after all, you can never tell where rain has been. The Cattermoles did not use their spider's web, in fact they took it down and put it in the garage, erecting instead two concrete posts at either end of the garden. Then a line appeared between the posts and on the line, at any hour of the day, on any day of the week, appeared the washing.

The spider webs are always situated near the

kitchen window in that secluded part of the garden where God created larch-lap fencing panels so that no one can be afflicted by the sight of neighbour's washing. But you could see Mrs Cattermole's washing as far along as Number 254, said my mother, who had apparently been there to find out. There was an outrageous volume of washing it seemed, metres of promiscuously flapping laundry; double sheets, bolster covers, baby's nappies—Mrs C did not do the decent thing and use disposables—and, worst of all, underwear. The Cattermoles were large, well-built people and their clothes were correspondingly large and well-built. When the washing filled with wind the thought of bosoms and bellies and buttocks and even barrage balloons was unavoidable.

My code name for the phenomenon was Big Knickers. If my mother was especially fretful when I came home from school, or snappish at breakfast, or downright shrewish on Sunday afternoons, I would murmur to myself, 'Big Knickers' and look out of the back windows, and I was always right.

It was Big Knickers the day after I discovered Old Compton. I was in a foul mood myself because last night, after finally getting home, I had written up my *Macbeth* notes and taken them round to Rowena.

'Keep them,' Rowena had said, barely answering the door when I rang her tubular bells, 'and don't imagine that you can come running to me next time you want something done.'

I slouched home wondering what she meant by 'next time', because I could not recall a single instance of Rowena ever having done me any favours, except detaching Peter Rafferty from me at a disco, and that only turned out to be a favour afterwards. Next morning I was still hanging about, so that I would not have to meet her on the way to school, when Karen Halford called round to collect my mother.

(They take turns to drive each other to work and call it their contribution to the Energy Crisis. Another contribution would be to catch the bus but this has never occurred to either of them.)

'Come and look at this,' Mum said, when the tubular bells began to chime and she went to let Karen in. At the patio door in the living room they stood and stared out over the garden.

'It's a bit much, isn't it?' Karen said, and I could hear teeth being sucked.

'It's always the same when the wind's in the west,' Mum said. 'I mean, if that line ran up the *middle* of their garden, it would be different, but he put it on *this* side of the path and it's much nearer to our fence. So when the wind comes from that direction a lot of that washing is blowing over the fence. It's actually on *our* side.'

'Mmmm. See what you mean. Of course, if it was a tree, you'd be legally entitled to cut it back. Have you approached the Residents' Association?'

I hadn't known that the real affront caused by the Big Knickers Syndrome was that Mrs Cattermole's washing was invading our air space.

'There was a private estate I was reading about, in Kent,' my mother was sighing. 'If you moved in there, the Residents' Association made you sign an undertaking not to hang out laundry on Tuesdays, Thursdays and weekends. And that was in the 1960s. You can't call it progress.'

'Why don't they use the rotary?'

'They put it in the garage.'

More sighing. 'Of course, with a tumble drier, it hardly matters about the drying area.' I loved 'drying area'.

'*She* doesn't have a tumbler.'

I began to think that they suspected Mrs Cattermole of getting some kind of vulgar kick from hang-

ing her bloomers to dry in public. I remembered
when our neighbours at the old place had Granny
and Grandpa over from Kashmir. Gran had disap-
proved of modern technology like washing lines, and
when she helped out with the laundry she draped it
neatly over the bushes in the front garden and Mrs
Khan was *mortified*.

'I suppose I could invite her round for coffee and
have a word . . .'

It was typical that she had not thought of inviting
Mrs Cattermole round for coffee before there was
something to complain about.

'I mean, what will happen in summer when we
want to sit in the garden and invite friends in? The
shadows will be on our lawn. Perhaps it would be
better to ask Brian to have a word with *him*.'

I tried to imagine Dad inviting Mr Cattermole to
join him in a pint at The Woolpack and confronting
him, man to man, about the D cups and Y fronts.

When at last I left the house, only just in time to
reach school, I found Mrs Cattermole walking down
the street ahead of me, wheeling baby Cattermole in
a buggy. As we approached the end of Coldharbour
I turned right and Mrs Cattermole turned left. She
saw me as we crossed the road and waved. I waved
back, feeling disloyal, not to Mum, for fraternizing
with the enemy, but to Mrs Cattermole. I liked her
and I had accidentally exposed her to scorn a few
weeks ago when I had shared the Big Knickers sce-
nario with some friends. I had been hoping that they
would find the situation as ridiculous as I did, but
instead they sympathized with Mum.

Lynzi gave me a funny look. 'It can't be very nice,'
she had said. 'People ought to keep their washing
private.' She was a true daughter of Compton
Rosehay.

Because I was anxious to avoid Rowena that morning I sat with Elaine Crossley at registration. This was not difficult because Elaine usually sat alone or with those indeterminate people who did not seem to belong to any particular group. I quite liked Elaine, especially that morning because she did not ask me why I had suddenly decided she was worth sitting with. She had been at the school for less than two terms and I did not know her very well; I did not even know where she lived. People, particularly VNPs, called her a swot, but she seemed to me to be effortlessly clever in a way I envied, as I spent my time effortfully trying not to seem clever at all. In spite of relying on my *Macbeth* notes, my maths assignments and my French translations, Rowena basically despised me for doing them. I was really very lucky to be allowed to be seen in the company of Rowena, Lynzi and Marie. Poor old Elaine had no luck at all in that respect, until this particular morning.

The lesson after registration was English which meant that we stayed in our own room and had a whole hour before we had to begin the daily routine of carrying everything we owned all over the school, along corridors, across quadrangles, up and down staircases, like people trying to climb Mount Everest without Sherpas or oxygen. Being Very Nice did not necessarily keep some people out of other people's lockers. In my first year at Lord John's only one locker on our corridor remained locked for an entire term, and that turned out to have a ham and pine-apple pizza in it.

I stayed on Elaine's table. I thought she might say something sarky like, 'To what do I owe this pleasure?' but she just behaved as though I always sat there and lent me a biro when mine ran out.

We were in different sets for maths, owing to Elaine's effortlessness. Rowena, Lynzi and Marie were in yet another set, a quiet undemanding crowd where they could sit in a corner and pass around their single brain cell, but we all had to head for the maths department and although I set off walking beside Elaine I discovered, half-way up the stairs, that she had somehow become separated from me, coralled would be a better word, and was now engulfed by Rowena, Lynzi and Marie who were chatting away, not so much to her as round her, as if they had just discovered how tremendously exciting she was to know. In a way, I suppose, they *had* only just discovered it. As I looked back Elaine caught my eye and rolled her own, under raised brows.

I took her to mean that she was not exactly thrilled by her new-found popularity, but when I ran into her in the cloakroom at lunch-time, she was still surrounded by her new friends.

'Coming to lunch?' I asked Elaine.

'We're going up to Manor Garth,' Rowena said. 'Enjoy your sandwiches,' she added, in case I had any ideas about going with them, but I hadn't. I very rarely went to Manor Garth for lunch, even when the others did, not to save money but as a matter of principle. When Compton Rosehay was first created, the food shops in the town centre had made it very clear that they did not want to be flooded with school kids at 12.30 every day, frightening the shoppers and making footprints on the pavements, and we had been forbidden to leave the school premises at lunch-time. Then the recession started to bite. Customers became very thin on the ground at any time of day and the shops all had a change of heart. The school had proved to have such an excellent reputation for courtesy, kindness, honesty and all-round jolly-good-showness, they said, that they would be perfectly happy to flog us fish and chips and pot noodles and kebabs. I don't know if the increase in takings balanced out the increase in shop-lifting, but there was no going back. It suited the staff to have the school half-empty for an hour as it saved them having to spend their lunch-breaks zipping round the field making sure that nobody got out.

Elaine went off with Rowena, Marie and Lynzi. I knew what they were up to and I wondered if she did. After being ignored by them for almost two terms she couldn't possibly imagine that they really wanted her company now; she must realize that she was just being used to get up my nose. On the other hand, they would have her undivided attention. I had never taken much notice of Elaine either. They could say anything they liked about me, and Elaine might well believe it. They could not have much else in common. Rowena had never been interested in Elaine because Elaine was not the kind of person that Rowena found interesting. She was heavily built, not quite on Cattermole lines but tall and solid and healthy. You could see at one glance that Elaine had never even thought about dieting. Rowena's chief topic of conversation was dieting, followed by lipo-suction and hair-styles. Marie would talk about lipo-suction but her real passion was silicone implants in the lips, and Lynzi subscribed to *Tattoo World* and collected information on body piercing. If they had one shared ambition it was to be able to fit into a size 8 at Miss Selfridge and cause bitter envy in the communal changing room. I never shopped any-where that had a communal changing room and I was much narrower than Elaine.

All because of *Macbeth*, I sulked, trailing alone to the canteen and the tables reserved for people who brought their own food, but I knew that it wasn't Macbeth's fault at all. It was Big Knickers all over again. The reason I liked Mrs Cattermole, I sus-pected, was that, deep down, I too was Big Knickers at heart, not really the sort of person who ought to be living in Compton Rosehay. What I really longed for were those gardens I saw from the train into London, full not only with lines of shameless under-wear and the unspeakable evidence that babies crap, but with old prams and hoses that people forgot to roll up neatly on their reels, if they had them, and unidentified lumps of concrete, slabs of breeze-block wall, bolted cabbages, sheets of corrugated iron, mat-tresses, paint cans, oil drums, sheds made of old railway sleepers, abandoned cars and dismembered motor bikes. I didn't want to live *in* one of those houses, I wanted access; to be able to walk through the streets where they stood, and perv into people's front windows, sneak up side alleys, discover ratty little parks with worn grass and broken swings; to hang out in a high street again or run to the corner shop in the rain, dodge traffic, scribble on posters in the bus shelter, queue for a bus that never came.

Buses in Compton Rosehay are like rides at a fair-ground. They appear at regular intervals, never late, round and round the town, clean and bright and smelling of computers. Nobody writes things in them, or scratches out letters so that they are *Licensed to eat 56 people*. If you miss one the next will be along in ten minutes. You can never use them as an excuse for being late because *they* are never late. They aren't real buses anyway, they look like converted ambu-lances. I haven't been on a double-decker bus since we left Stoke Newington.

While I was picking over my sandwiches a thought struck me. I *did* have access to grunge if I wanted it; not 100% London grunge, but the rural variety. All I had to do to get my fix was to walk home again through Old Compton. It wasn't really what I wanted because the sort of places I had in mind were heaving with life, life that was getting out of hand

24

(the sort of life that in the end drives people to murder each other), and Old Compton was on its death bed, but it was better than nothing. No toy buses ran down that street.

We had science all afternoon and I didn't see Elaine again until the final bell rang (it isn't a real bell but the sort of electronic whoop you get with Red Alert on the Star Ship *Enterprise*). I didn't see her because she was surrounded by Rowena for the whole double period, with Marie and Lynzi nipping at her ankles like a couple of sheepdogs in case she got away. They herded her into the cloakroom, along the corridor, down the drive. When they reached the gate there was a conference of some kind and then they all moved off towards Manor Garth. I saw Rowena turn her head and give me a long look. I stopped dead, as if struck by a sudden thought, and ran back into the building, pretending to have forgotten something. When I came out again they were no longer in sight. No one—no one who mattered—would see me walk down the drive and, as I had done yesterday, turn left. Taking the sinister side, I thought, sinisterly.

And I thought, as I walked, that I had never liked Rowena anyway, which was true, and that I didn't care what she thought of me or what she might tell Elaine, which was not. And the real reason I had stopped there on the drive, was that what I really feared when I turned left at the gate was that they would follow me. I wished they had not seen me yesterday. I didn't want anyone else to find Old Compton, although a lot of people must know that it was there. There must be several houses in Compton Rosehay that overlooked that sad little street, or at least its roofs. Did no one wonder or did no one care?

I hurried down the alley. Yesterday had been overcast; today the sun was shining. Beyond the bollards at the far end of the alley I could see a patch of bright leaves. It was spring. Soon in Compton Rosehay the hanging baskets would come out of hibernation and hang themselves, full of petunias and lobelias and trailing ivy, upside down like floral bats outside people's porches and from the lamp posts in Manor Garth. Window boxes outside The Woolpack, The Drovers and The Dog and Partridge would sprout geraniums. Robin Hood would stand his bay trees in tubs on the pavement. I hoped very much that Mrs Cattermole would have dandelions on her lawn, and bindweed growing up the posts of her wanton washing line.

On Wednesday I too had been overcast, so shadowed by the sadness of Old Compton that I hadn't noticed what it had going for it. With the conifer hedge concealing the town on one side and the grassy embankment of the ring road on the other, Old Compton hid in its own valley. Fruit trees were coming into flower in back gardens, hedges were breaking into leaf. I could hear someone using a lawnmower somewhere, not an electric or petrol machine, but the old-fashioned cylinder kind that whirred and clacked.

I could smell cut grass. I wandered for a while on a patch of wasteland where a few wild flowers were growing. I looked in at the window of the old post office and read the notices that still hung there, for an Easter Beetle Drive at the village hall; a garden party at the Vicarage, Rosehay; a Harvest Supper; a coach trip to London for Christmas shopping. A whole year was preserved in that window.

The postcards in the glass case were almost illegible. *For sale: Green lady's bycicle. Three speed. Ten pound's. Found: Ginger kitten, white feet. Apply within.* I was so relieved that the notice said found and not lost. I knew I should have cried again at the thought of that long-ago lost kitten, wondering if it had ever come home. I hoped that the green lady had managed to sell her bicycle.

In towns (not in Compton Rosehay of course) when shops close, flyposters come by night and stick political slogans and adverts for rock concerts all over the windows. No one had done that in Old Compton. I could see into the empty supermarket through the dirty glass, to the abandoned shelves and freezers, a dusty counter where a cash till still stood, fading advertisements for cheap offers, two for one, unbeatable value, one week only.

Once more the only sign of life was the house where yesterday I had heard music and seen Big Knickers. The doors were open again and the washing had gone, so that in the back garden I could see apple trees in blossom. Compton Rosehay trees always have trusses of flowers in the spring, but never seem to produce any fruit. Fruit grows in polythene bags, everyone knows that.

I crossed the road, as I had done yesterday, to look in the antique shop, feeling self-conscious as I stepped out from the shelter of the privet hedge. Perhaps someone would look out from an upstairs window of the live house and see by my school uniform that I was a vile interloper. Was there anyone left in Old Compton young enough to go to school, old enough to go to Lord John's? Surely they would look different, the way I had imagined adults from Old Compton would look different in Manor Garth. They would resemble draggly orphans from old books, surely, with boots that didn't fit, stringy hair, jackets too tight, sleeves too short, skirts too long.

Since last night a new item had appeared in the window of the antique shop. It was a small alabaster block, about the size and colour of a pound of medium Cheddar, and embedded in it was a brass

27

thing, that looked vaguely Aztec, with three smaller brass things dangling from it. I liked it because it proved that there was life in the antique shop, the will to sell was still flickering. Someone was proud of the object, they had put it right in the front of the window, the brass had been polished. I could see what it was meant to be *now*, a paperweight or a pen stand, something to do with writing in ink on leather-topped wooden bureaux, but what had it been *once*? That was its chief charm. It had not been created *whole*, like Compton Rosehay, traditionally hand-crafted by God; it had been put together. Someone had bored holes in the alabaster and fitted the brass thing into it. It had a vaguely religious look, I thought, and as I was thinking it, I felt someone beside me, and a voice said, 'The Martians left it.'

— 3 —
Earth's Fabric

'You what?' I said, and turned. Elaine Crossley was standing beside me, also looking at the thing in the window. My first thought was to check and make sure that she did not have Rowena, Lynzi and Marie concealed about her person.

'It was left behind by the Martians,' Elaine said. She was alone. It was safe to go on thinking while I spoke instead of operating on auto-pilot as you had to at school where saying something sincere or original could ruin your reputation.

'I thought it might have come out of a church,' I said.

'Or a temple. Of course, you know they were missionaries.'

'The Martians were missionaries?'

'Forget all that rubbish about galactic domination,' Elaine said, matter-of-factly. 'They came to save us. They were terrible bores, but they were never dangerous.'

'I suppose they held revivalist meetings in their space ship?'

'At first,' Elaine said, 'but then they built a small tin tabernacle. That was in the days before religious persecution set in.'

'One of those chapels along here?' I said, pointing down the street.

'No.' Elaine gestured vaguely towards the silhouette of the distant conifer hedge. 'Up there in Stalemate.'

Why had I never known before that Compton Rosehay was really called Stalemate? What I did know, there and then, was that Elaine Crossley was far too valuable to be left in the care of Rowena's mob. It was a matter of extreme urgency.

'Think about it,' Elaine went on, 'if the Martians had come as conquerors they'd have built huge imperialistic monuments all over Stalemate. There would be triumphal arches over the ring road and a Palace of Culture in the shopping centre.' She turned and looked again at the thing in the window. 'Obviously, that's a holy relic.'

'What did they do with it?'

'The Martians? Reverenced it, probably. Doesn't it strike you as odd that there are so many chapels round here?'

'This must be the religious quarter. Were the Martians Christians?'

'Oh, no. Evangelical pagans. Idolators—that's one of their idols—'

'Why the chapels, then?'

'Ah, but they weren't chapels to begin with, were they? You know how early Christians used to take over pagan temples and annex pagan festivals—'

'What, like Yule becoming Christmas?'

'Exactly. They took over the Martians, too. Why should it be different in Stalemate?'

I was beginning to think that things were very different in Stalemate. 'I didn't realize that that was its real name.' I had to keep her going. I think I understood then that she was quite as desperate as I was, and after only five months.

'It depends what you mean by reality,' Elaine said. 'Let's walk down to my place.'

I knew immediately where she lived, which was her place. No wonder I had never seen her around town. We headed for the house of the Big Knickers.

Elaine said, as we walked along, 'This place that is called Compton Rosehay, it's really there. It exists.

We walk through it. Our real feet strike its real pavements. The houses cast real shadows, they blot out the sun.'

'The same sun that shines on Lord John Randyll's, the Manor Garth, on The Mucky Duck. We see what's there—'

'But what we see isn't all that's there.'

'Virtual reality?'

'Alternative reality. Compton Rosehay is there and we're in it.'

'A sort of overlay—wait a minute. *This* isn't Compton Rosehay. We're in *Old* Compton.'

'I'm coming to that,' said Elaine. 'Don't you notice the difference the minute you leave Old Compton Street, go up the slip road or along the alley? Old Compton is three-dimensional, but this is all there is—what we can see. Up in Compton Rosehay—'

'Hang on,' I said, 'are we talking Fourth Dimension here?'

'Not quite, more *double* dimensions; like you said, an overlay. Compton Rosehay is there and so is Stalemate.'

We stopped at Elaine's front gate. I heard music again.

'You mean they occupy the same space?'

'Exactly, but no one is aware of it.'

'Except us.'

'This street is one of the places where the real world shows through.'

'There's a few places up there, too,' I said, thinking of the relics of Rosehay.

'But most of the time Compton Rosehay goes about its horrible business and never realizes that it shares space and time with Stalemate. What we've got here in Old Compton is an interstice. Earth's fabric has worn thin.'

'That sounds like *Macbeth*,' I said, as we walked up the path to Elaine's front door.

'Earth's fabric *hath* worn thin and so we see the other where beneath.'

'Do you think Shakespeare knew about alternative reality?'

'Sure he did,' Elaine said.

There were no tubular bells by Elaine's front door.

'Can I use your phone—let Mum know I'll be late?'

'Go ahead. Then come up to the attic,' Elaine said. She called out to someone unseen, 'Charlotte's going to ring home,' and then bounded up the uncarpeted stairs that twanged and squeaked as her feet hit each tread.

I picked up the handset hesitantly, but no answering voice demanded, 'Who's Charlotte? Has she got a rotary clothesline? Can she get into a size 8?' The only sounds were a distant hammering and the music, old Beatles records today. No one came out to see what kind of a visitor was being allowed to walk on the fitted carpet. There was no carpet, only a runner with frayed edges, rolled up at one end where people had been tripping over it for years.

I made my call, explained that I was with a friend but not explaining which friend, and followed Elaine upstairs. On the landing a man was sawing the banisters in half, but he looked up, nodded pleasantly and indicated the next flight, to the attic. I passed an open door and looked in to see an empty bedroom with a tent pitched in it. A pair of naked male feet—they *are* a different shape from ours—was sticking out at one end.

Elaine's attic was almost as bare as the camp site; again, no carpet, a single bed, an old cane chair and a dozen tea chests stacked against the wall. Two other tea chests, with a rug across the top, forming a divan, stood under the window which looked out over the back garden and the conifer hedge, the boundary of Stalemate.

'We could never have lived *in* Stalemate,' Elaine said. 'They'd have run us out of town on a rail. What did you tell your mother—not the truth, I hope.'

'I said I was having tea with a friend. I expect she thought I meant Rowena.'

'She won't *mind* you coming here, will she?'

'She doesn't know Old Compton exists. I don't think anyone does.'

'Rowena does,' Elaine said. 'She knows now. She asked me where I lived, so I told her. "Oh," she said, "those derelict houses down by the ring road. They're condemned." After that she didn't mind a bit when I said I had to go home. She kept saying, "But you aren't going to *stay* there, are you?" Well, we aren't, actually, but not for the reason she thinks.'

'Not staying?' Now I came to think of it the house looked as if it was occupied by people who had been there five days rather than five months. I remembered the tent in the room below. 'When are you going?'

'I don't know, we're only renting. John—my father—that guy on the landing sawing the house down, he's a civil engineer.' She lowered her voice. 'We don't talk about this, but he's working on a motorway interchange. Usually if anyone asks we say he's an embezzler. One has to hold up one's head.'

I had always thought that a civil engineer was a respectable thing to be, well, civil, at any rate.

'Oh, it is,' Elaine said, 'but things are different since the flyover entered our lives. This interchange is going to make Spaghetti Junction look like mere noodles. We're hoping for something morally defensible next time, like a suspension bridge. The trouble is, every time he changes jobs we all have to move;

well, we don't; we could all stay put, but we like to be with him. We like Old Compton too, but we like him better, and we'd like Old Compton even more if it didn't have Stalemate attached to it.'

'But why did you come here?'

'We got a map and a pair of compasses,' Elaine said, 'and put the point on the flyover and drew a circle round it to discover how far away from it we could afford to live.'

'You'll go mad with boredom,' I predicted. 'I don't know why you aren't mad with boredom already.'

'Why should I be bored?' Elaine said. 'I'm never bored by myself.'

'Nor am I,' I said, but it wasn't true. I needed other people, almost as if the fact that they noticed me proved that I existed. Could it really be the case that Elaine needed only herself?

'The compass factor is very important in the annals of Stalemate,' I said, savouring the name. 'God, you know . . . the basic design.' I explained my Creation theory.

'I thought he did it with a pastry cutter,' Elaine said.

Elaine's mother called up that the kettle had boiled if we wanted tea, so we went down, past Mr Crossley who was carrying away a whole section of the banister rail. The feet were still poking out of the tent.

'Who . . . ?'

'My brother Paul,' Elaine said. 'Down from Newcastle for the vac. He's here so little that it's not worth getting any furniture out of storage for him. With that tent and a sleeping bag he doesn't even need a heater. And spring is coming. Up in Stalemate the bog asset-stripper is bursting into flower and the song of the sheep can be heard in the land. You knew, I suppose, that the sheep of Stalemate are renowned for their melody. Infatuated naturalists hide all night in the bushes with recording equipment, making tapes. Poets write odes; you know; "Bliss was it in that dawn to be alive, but to be a sheep was very heaven!" '

I was beginning to see why Elaine had spent two terms at Lord John's without speaking to anyone. Who could she have spoken to?

By the time we reached the kitchen, which was big and warm and fully furnished, Elaine's mother was out in the garden. Elaine made tea and assembled sandwiches by enclosing a cream cracker between two slices of cheese.

'It cuts down on crumbs,' Elaine said. She opened the window to put a mug of tea on the sill outside, waving to her mother who came to collect it with earthy hands and a trowel tucked into a pocket of her smock. It was the first time I had seen her, a big, slow-moving woman, fit occupant for the washing that yesterday had billowed over the garden. 'What are you planting, Marge?' Elaine said.

'Carrots,' Mrs Crossley said, wandering away again with the mug.

'That's the saddest thing,' Elaine said, watching her go. 'Whenever we move she starts gardening. If it's autumn she puts bulbs in, in spring she sows vegetables. It's an act of faith—that one day we'll be in the same place long enough to pick the flowers or harvest the crop. Well, we got the daffodils—if we go before the carrots come up, promise that you'll come down and harvest them. Remember us when you eat them.'

I was becoming depressed by all this talk of moving on. Already I wanted Elaine to stay for ever so that we could explore Stalemate together. After this, how could I go back to discussing cellulite with Rowena?

'I ought to be going soon,' I said reluctantly, at half

past six. At the back of my mind I was developing the feeling that as soon as I left Elaine's house the light would go out and the place return to dereliction, so that when I looked back there would be no curtains at the windows, no music drifting over the garden, no washing, no carrots; and that when I mentioned Elaine at school next day Rowena would look vague and say, honestly mystified, '*Who*? Who are you talking about?'

'I'll walk round with you,' Elaine said, 'unless you're catching a bus. Legs in Compton Rosehay are mutating into vestigial fins, which accounts for the prevalence of mermaids in Stalemate, but that's another story.'

We waved goodbye to Mrs Crossley through the window and went out into the hall where Mr Crossley was hanging over the remains of the banisters with a plumb-line.

'He has to keep his hand in,' Elaine said, 'or his engineering skills might atrophy overnight and then what would happen to the flyover? The Government's entire transport policy would collapse.' Somewhere higher up a male voice, Paul's, I supposed, was singing along to the Beatles:

I thought I'd lost my mind but I saw it yesterday-ay.
I'm not the hurting kind, but they're putting me away-
　　ay,
Because I'm barmy, and I know you think I'm mad,
Yeah-yeah-yeah . . .

The sun had long ago sunk behind the false horizon of the ring road embankment and as we walked back down the street towards the alley-way the last of the light was leaving the sky as it set invisibly, a second time. Elaine, evidently accustomed to saying nothing, said nothing. I was trying to visualize a map of Compton Rosehay according to the Crossley projection. I no longer saw it as a tea tray, more as a pancake flexibly conforming to the contours of what lay beneath, except where Stalemate shouldered through and, like many pancakes, a little ragged at one edge, revealing the three simple dimensions of Old Compton.

'Is this the boundary?' I asked, when we reached the mouth of the alley-way which had become a chute of draughty shadows, 'or is it at the other end?'

'Earth's fabric is badly frayed here,' Elaine said, after a moment's consideration which took us several metres up the alley and into the shadows. 'Only the initiated, which is us, can tell exactly when they leave and enter Stalemate; a certain miasma in the air on the way up, a balmy fragrance on the way down . . .'

We came in sight of the sports hall which, being so much higher than Old Compton Street, caught the afterglow on its iron flanks and loured over us. It boomed and clanged hollowly from some kind of ball game going on inside.

Elaine said, with conviction, 'Why, *this* is Stalemate, nor am I out of it.'

'Shakespeare?'

'Marlowe.'

'Who?'

'Christopher Marlowe, Kit to his friends, that-two-faced-bugger-who-works-for-MI5 to everyone else. You know who I mean, the gay spy poet; wrote *Doctor Faustus* and died in a punch-up in a pub. That's how I like my poets. Someone stabbed him through the eye. None of that wandering lonely as a cloud nonsense.'

'I thought he was an Elizabethan,' I said, feebly.

'Listen, kid, Good Queen Bess *invented* MI5. Haven't you heard of Sir Francis Walsingham? Walsingham's Men made our lot look like pussy-cats. Walsingham would have had James Bond hung up

39

on a meat hook with boiling lead in his ears while his entrails were winched out. When Walsingham said, "I'll have your guts for garters", he meant it.'

I could see that I was going to have my work cut out if I was to remain worthy of admission to Stalemate. Elaine *thought* so fast.

We were passing the school. Its full name is Lord John Randyll's Comprehensive School and Community College, which means that after school ends everyone else in the town can use the facilities. People were then arriving in cars, and a few on foot, for aerobics sessions and gymnastics and evening classes in beauty and fitness. I think a lot of them believed that you could become beautiful and fit just by turning up. Under their coats they were all smooth and shiny in lycra, like tropical lizards.

'The Martians,' Elaine murmured, 'are holding one of their giant revivalist meetings.'

'*Those* are the Martians?'

'No, no, the Martians are already inside, rejoicing on the podium,' Elaine said. 'I told you they were missionaries. They arrived in Stalemate very early one morning in a matt-black capsule and after a brief prayer and laying-on of hands—they had four each so it took a little while—they spread out all over Stalemate, knocking on people's doors, handing out leaflets and singing Hallelujah. Tonight they've flown in a spectacular preacher who speaks in tongues and the whole population is flocking to hear him.'

'It's aerobics,' I said.

'That's how it appears to the outside world. You've heard of Shakers, Quakers, Holy Rollers. At Martian services the congregation performs ritualized movements to discordant music, rolling around on small prayer mats and waving their legs in the air. Call it aerobics if you like,' Elaine said; 'we know better. When they come out afterwards they are all glowing and convinced that they've been Saved. Death has been driven back another twenty-four hours because their muscles are full of air. So are their heads. Aerobics is the opium of the people.'

'I thought you said the Martians were terrible bores.'

'Have you ever tried talking to a fitness freak?' Elaine said. We had left the school far behind now and the aerobic music was fading into the distance. Of course I had tried talking to a fitness freak.

'Did Rowena say anything to you about liposuction?' I asked, although the only kind of fit that Rowena cared about was, as I said, size 8 at Miss Selfridge.

'Isn't that where they syphon off all your surplus fat and leave your empty thighs flapping in the breeze? Can't you imagine the effect afterwards, these flabby paddles of drained *skin* slapping damply against each other when you walk along?'

'What I want to know,' I said, 'is what they do with the fat. I saw it done on television once. It comes out liquid and goes into a bottle . . .'

'Which is immediately sealed, dated and put into a fat bank for sale at exorbitant prices to people who are too thin. There is an international fat compatability register. Of course, it's different here in Stalemate. A lot of the bottles are purloined by venal liposuction operatives and sold for cash to the mermaid factory.'

'There is a mermaid *factory*?'

'You know that big iron barn place at the end of Old Compton Street, just opposite the bus stop at the top of the slip road.'

'Where it says O GLEE..?'

'That's the place.'

'It's got old petrol pumps outside; I think it used to be a garage.'

'You may think so,' Elaine said, 'but remember,

here in Stalemate what you see is not necessarily what is there. Earth's fabric hath worn thin. The real Stalemate is all around us, but we only get occasional glimpses of it. You'll just have to take it on trust. It's a mermaid factory.'

— 4 —
Party-Plan
in Stalemate

I wondered what the Gang of Three would do next morning; probably lie in wait to ignore us. Ignoring someone at Lord John's was not merely a matter of taking no notice. That was too unreliable; it was quite possible that the person who was being ignored would not notice that they were having no notice taken of them. What I expected to happen was that Rowena, Lynzi and Marie would make sure that they were somewhere around when I arrived, and then talk to each other loudly as though I were not there, not to suggest that they hadn't seen me but to make sure that I knew I was being seen—much in the way one sees a pane of glass, you know it's there but you don't actually look at it, only through it. That's how they would treat me, like a pane of dirty glass, something slightly, but not seriously, in the way. I wasn't sure how they would manage with Elaine. Up until yesterday they had never taken any notice of Elaine anyway.

It might be that, since discovering that Elaine lived beyond the Pale, in Old Compton, Rowena had made up her mind overnight that she was hardly worth the bother of getting to know any better. Then again, she might see that Elaine was back in my company and decide that Elaine would have to be detached once more. Would it be worth the effort to annoy me if it resulted in lumbering herself with someone she didn't want to be seen dead with? I felt almost sorry for Rowena. It must be hell living such a complicated life. Why not just settle for being miserable, like me? With GCSE coming up I wondered that she had enough spare brain cells left to devote to the problem of working out who to sit next to.

Apart from avoiding Rowena again on the way to school, I decided not to do anything different from usual. Why should Rowena force me into the same kind of contortions just because she enjoyed tying herself in knots? I went straight to the classroom and sat at the table that didn't matter. Elaine had not arrived yet so I had a chance to look at the other people who didn't matter. They looked quite normal. In fact, all that was wrong with them was that they didn't matter to Rowena. It was odd; I worked with them, played sport with them, talked to them in queues, even joined them at Jangles Coffee House in Manor Garth, sometimes. Mary Sinclaire, over there; I had even got out videos and gone to her house for the evening, but Rowena had let it be understood that she *didn't matter* so we had never become friends. Over the last day or two I had been asking myself why Rowena should matter. She was lazy, unkind, sour, but she had always understood one thing—the value of the pre-emptive strike. While other people could happily spend weeks, months, whole terms, years even, sizing each other up and eventually finding that they were friends (I supposed too that unless you were daft enough to go in for love at first sight, this was how you ended up marrying somebody— because they were still there) Rowena got in first and gave orders, drew up battle plans and took no prisoners. Friendship with extreme prejudice was how Rowena operated.

While I sat on the corner table, not mattering, Rowena, Lynzi and Marie came and occupied their table. There was an empty chair at it—mine. Without looking in my direction Lynzi hooked her foot under one of the rungs and propelled it away from the table towards the wall. My death warrant.

I was so busy watching all this that I did not notice Elaine come in until she dropped her bag and books on the table beside me.

'Have you ever tried Zen yoghurt?' Elaine said.

'Tried what?' It was a good start. I didn't even have to worry about saying hello.

'In the Manor Garth there's a shop that sells Zen yoghurt. Haven't you seen it?'

'That's Jangles Coffee House,' I said. 'They put the new espresso machine in front of the advert. It's frozen yoghurt.'

'Earth's fabric . . .' Elaine said. 'It may be frozen yoghurt in Compton Rosehay but we know better. Zen yoghurt is a celebrated delicacy in Stalemate, fermented from the milk of the harmonious sheep and flavoured with prohibited substances. It's a psy-chedelicacy, actually,' she added, with a flash of inspiration. I wished I could do that.

'*Are* any substances prohibited in Stalemate?'

'They live by a code as rigid as anything in the Western world,' Elaine said, severely.

'So what do they put in the yoghurt?'

'I'll tell you later. I've got Latin and economics for the rest of the morning. Do you want to eat here at lunch-time or go in search of unheard-of experiences?'

'Go in search of unheard-of experiences,' I said, assuming she meant the Manor Garth.

'Right, we'll go back to my place.'

It seemed that we were as likely to have unheard-of experiences in Old Compton as anywhere else. I spent the rest of the morning being seen through by the Gang of Three, recalling glumly that the four of us had actually sat down and planned to take the same GCSE options irrespective of what we enjoyed or what we were good at. I even had time, during art, to come to the conclusion that since this bright idea had been, it goes without saying, Rowena's, what had probably happened was that she had worked out all the things she was bad at and made sure that one of the other three of us would be in a position to do them for her. Maths, French and English Literature had been my contribution to the scheme. It occurred to me, at the same time, that as I was no longer under any obligation to make my work available to Rowena it would be worth my while to make an extra effort, since I would be the only one to benefit.

Elaine was waiting for me at the end of the morning, on the landing of the CDT block.

'Ready?' I said, swinging my bag briskly. I could feel waves of indifference surging up the corridor behind me from the Gang of Three.

'Just a minute,' Elaine said. She was staring out of the window above the stairs.

'Have you got somebody under surveillance?'

'In a manner of speaking. What's that street that runs along the side of the field?'

'That one there? Shepway.'

'See that little guy on the bike—watch where he goes.'

A man on a sit-up-and-beg bicycle was coming down Shepway. At the fifth house along from the Tithe Barn Lane end, the left hand one of a pair, he got off the bicycle, wheeled it up the path and vanished along a side entry.

'What about him?'

'I've noticed him three or four times,' Elaine said. 'Room 3K looks out this way, where we have economics.' We went down the stairs, two flights, and out on to the side path that ran round to the front drive. 'The point is, although I always see him come out of the sixth house, when he comes back he always goes into the fifth.'

The only remotely interesting thing about Shepway as far as the school was concerned was that Wheeler the Dealer hung out at Number 41, but you didn't go there in daylight. 'Perhaps they share a drive, or an entrance or something.'

'No, they don't. They're semi-detached. The entrances are on opposite sides.'

'Perhaps he's identical twins. Perhaps he isn't the same man anyway—it's just two blokes with the same kind of bike. I mean, you haven't been using a telescope, have you? Those houses are a long way away.'

'Look, Charlotte, you've got to stop trying to find rational explanations for everything,' Elaine said, more in sorrow than in anger. 'That is Clyster the bigamist we've been watching.'

As we reached the sports hall and turned the corner I looked back at Shepway. There were houses on one side of the street only, so it was the fronts that faced the school field. From one room or another, from the hockey pitch and the tennis courts, I had been looking at the fronts of those houses for three years. Why had I never noticed what was going on? For the same reason, probably, that I had never wondered what lay beyond the conifer hedge. The conifer hedge was there to stop you wondering; in Compton Rosehay, what you saw was what you got. Not any longer . . .

Mr George Clyster, the bigamist, lived in Number 5 and Number 6 Shepway. Every night at ten o'clock he said goodbye to Mrs Clyster I and his strapping daughter Mavis and left the house, Number 6, carefully closing the gate behind him and waving to the women as they stood at the door watching him cycle up the road, until he reached the end and turned left into Copsewood. He then proceeded along Copsewood, turned left again into The Furlong, and left into The Spinney, which led into Tithe Barn Lane. Here he turned left yet again, continued along Tithe Barn Lane until he found himself at the corner of Shepway, made a final left turn and dismounted at the gate of Number 5. He wheeled his bicycle into the back garden and went into the kitchen where Mrs Clyster II was waiting with a tempting supper. They sat in front of the television to eat it, washed up together, put out the milk bottles, locked the doors and retired to bed where Mr Clyster did what a man's gotta do and then fell into an untroubled sleep.

Next morning he rose refreshed, ate breakfast with Mrs Clyster II and the three little Clysters, Lucy, Ben and Emma, kissed them all goodbye and wheeled his bicycle out of the side entry and rode away *down* Shepway. This time he turned right into Tithe Barn Lane, right again into The Spinney, then into The Furlong, along Copsewood and finally right again to ride home down Shepway, stopping this time at Number 6, where Mavis and Mrs Clyster I were waiting for him with a second breakfast. Then he went to bed where he remained until it was time to get up, eat dinner with Mrs Clyster I and Mavis, leave the house at ten o'clock and start the whole business over again.

Both Mrs Clysters believed that he worked shifts at the mermaid factory—

'Hang on,' I said. 'And don't tell me I'm being rational, but this isn't going to work. He can't have a job at all. He spends twenty-one hours a day in bed.'

'He's the local blackmailer,' Elaine said, without hesitation. 'It's obvious when you come to think of it. In a town like Stalemate the pickings would be enormous. I can't imagine why no one else has thought of it.'

'But they have,' I said. 'There's far too much going on here for *one* blackmailer to handle. There must be a sort of consortium.'

'Maybe they're all at it. Party-plan sessions; you know; you get the blackmail concession for your street and then ask the neighbours round—'

'And offer them victims—'

'No, *they* are the victims. What you offer is the chance—no, opportunity—to have their secrets kept safe at very affordable rates.'

'Is Clyster doing party-plan? I thought that kind of thing was aimed at housewives who wanted to earn a bit on the side.' The classified pages in the local rag were full of ads for party-plan agents; everything from kitchen appliances to sex-aids.

'I should imagine Clyster's back at Head Office,' Elaine said. 'Of course, you know what's going to happen, don't you? The mermaid factory will suddenly switch to the three-shift system. Clyster will have to acquire a third wife.'

'This could get out of hand,' I objected. 'How is it that the various Mrs Clysters have failed to notice each other? Doesn't Mrs Clyster II ever look out of her living room window, or stroll down to the shops, and see her old man wheeling his bike up somebody else's side entrance or waving goodbye to the next door neighbours?'

'It's the neighbourliness that enables him to get away with it,' Elaine explained. 'He is well known in the street for his little unthinking acts of kindness. People are accustomed to seeing him popping in and out of each other's houses to fix leaky washers and paint barge boards and clear out infestations.'

'I still think it could get out of control,' I said dubiously. 'What about Mrs Clyster III? You have to admit it's not a common name. Doesn't it strike any of them as odd that there should be so many Clysters in one street?'

'You were very close to the truth earlier on when you mentioned identical twins,' Elaine said. 'In fact Mr George Clyster passes himself off as a multiple birth.'

'He's *triplets*?'

'Quads, actually.'

'You mean, there's a fourth Mrs Clyster?'

'Not as yet,' Elaine said, 'but Mr Clyster is a man of parts.'

'Several parts,' I said.

'Don't be vulgar. It may, in the future, be necessary or desirable for Mr Clyster to lead himself to the altar for a fourth time. Since no factory, even in Stalemate, would operate a four-shift system, he has been in the habit of dropping hints about a long-lost brother, separated from the others at birth. Dammit, the man's a blackmailer. Do you seriously expect him to be honest and loyal?'

Mr Crossley was off building his flyover when we reached the house, and Elaine's mother was out. Paul, the owner of the feet in the tent, was alone in the kitchen eating Crossley cheese sandwiches and looking gloomily at a letter.

'Not a rejection slip?' Elaine said, sympathetically.

'I wouldn't mind a slip,' Paul said, looking up. He was big, like Elaine, but lean. I'd guessed as much from his feet. 'A rejection *slip* would be objective, clinical, over in seconds. I wouldn't even have to read it. But they *will* write letters, all sorrowful and enthusiastic, saying that my work doesn't fit their list at the present time.'

'Have you written a book?' I asked him, even though we hadn't been introduced.

'Poetry,' Elaine said, as Paul's mouth was full of

cheese again. 'But no one wants to publish it. How far down the list are you?'

'Three more small presses to try,' Paul said. '*Small* small presses, that is. I've done the big small presses. It will be the tiny weeny small presses next. After that I shall be reduced to selling it on street corners.'

We stood around in the kitchen eating cheese while Elaine tried to console Paul. I thought of my friends' big brothers, who treated their younger sisters as a lower life form or made remarks that would have got them run in for sexual harassment at work, if they brought friends home with them. Paul talked to Elaine as if she was just another person, he talked to *me* as if I was just another person. I wondered if he knew about Stalemate.

'When did you first try to get published?' I asked him casually.

'When was it, Lainey?' he said. 'September? October?'

'November,' Elaine said. 'Just after we came here.'

I caught her eye. We mouthed 'Stalemate' at each other. It had to be the effect of living so close to Stalemate that was causing Paul's failure to be published. I was fairly sure that there were no authors living in Compton Rosehay. What would they write about?

Elaine motioned me over to the window.

'He doesn't know,' she said quietly, 'and we won't let on. Stalemate is our dreadful secret. Tell you what, after school let's go up to the Manor Garth and eat Zen yoghurt, enhanced as it is by essence of stockbroker's nightshade. Who knows what may be revealed unto us.'

By seven o'clock the streets of Compton Rosehay were empty.

'It's like walking in Limbo,' Elaine said. 'Where does everybody get to?'

'In suspended animation till morning?' I suggested.

'They might at least be out exercising their familiars.'

'When we lived in Stoke Newington I used to hang out round the cemetery with Aneesa Khan from next door.'

'Is there a cemetery here? Do people die?'

'They just get recycled,' I said. 'You know the bottle bank in the car park, back of Sainsbury's. Well, there's a body bank, too.'

'That sounds more like Stalemate to me,' Elaine said. 'A story for which the world is not yet prepared. Now, see what I mean about familiars? Look at that guy over there.'

Sauntering down Copsewood was a lone pedestrian, the first we had seen since we left Jangles, accompanied by a black retriever with white whiskers round its muzzle.

'That's Mr Lomax, Head of Lower School,' I said. 'He teaches German.'

'I thought I'd seen him around. And who is that with him?'

'*Who*? That's his dog. I don't know what it's called.'

'It has no name—and Lomax is only the handle by which the world knows its owner.'

As far as I could see Mr Lomax was strolling peacefully along the street with the dog ambling at his heels. Very few of our teachers lived in Compton Rosehay; sensibly they arrived by car from long distances each morning at 8.30, but Mr Lomax had a house in Restharrow and his children were at one of the middle schools. He waved vaguely at us, recognizing me at least, and continued along the pavement, not looking back to see that Elaine was staring after him. Elaine did not take German.

'The dog, of course,' Elaine said, 'is a soul-hound.'

I thought she said 'sole' hound. 'Shoes, you mean?' I had confused notions of aniseed and tracker dogs.

'No, soul, as in body and. Lord Tod collects corpses from the body bank. That pair of scavengers collect what's left.'

'Lomax is all right,' I said, defensively.

'Not if he lives in Stalemate.' Elaine was firm. 'He may have been all right once, but now his heart is turned entirely to cheese. Captain Cheeseheart is feared and loathed the length and breadth of Stalemate.'

I turned for a last look at Captain Cheeseheart and his soul-hound. German lessons would never be the same again.

'But who's Lord Tod?'

'The corpse collector.'

'Yes, but *who*? Would we know him if we saw him?'

'*We* would. Thousands wouldn't. He lives at the manor, naturally. He's lord of it.'

'But there isn't a manor,' I said, 'only the Manor Garth and you know what that is. It's as phoney as everything else. I've seen the maps in the library. There never was a manor house.'

'What do you mean, *was*?' Elaine said, reprovingly. '*Is. Is.* The manor of Stalemate still stands. Lord Tod stalks his demesne.'

'Unseen—'

'Unrecognized. When he prowls his leafy avenues people see only the manager of Sainsbury's, strolling past the cooked-meats gondola, but we know better. Remember Earth's fabric. What people see is not necessarily what is there . . .'

— 5 —
The Logic of the Lawyer Jones

Sainsbury Tod inherited the lordship of the manor in a fashion which would have caused raised eyebrows and possibly criminal proceedings anywhere else, but was taken very much for granted in Stalemate. Young Sainsbury was a computer polisher. As far as he knew his origins were as humble as his employment, and although his father had often hinted that the family was distantly connected to the Tods of Stalemate he had always put this down to wishful thinking. Then, one morning, in the mail, he perceived a long legal envelope among the bills on the doormat. His first thought was that he was being sued for not paying somebody something, but when he finally brought himself to open it he discovered a communication from the lawyer Jones, writing under the letterhead of the Stalemate Blackmail Co-operative, and announcing that he had a small proposition to lay before Sainsbury Tod which might be to their mutual advantage.

Tod, immediately assuming that the proposition involved parting with large sums of money on a regular basis, began to cast his mind back over anything he had ever done which might now be about to land him in a blackmailer's clutches. After three hours, by which time he ought to have been at work among his computers, he had failed to come up with any crime, error or omission. As far as he knew he had led a blameless life. He cleared away the breakfast things, brewed a pot of black coffee and sat down to list everything he had ever done that had appeared blameless at the time but might look culpable in the

cold light of day. The following morning he went
out and bought an A4 notepad of two hundred sheets
and began to record everything he had ever done of
any description, and he was still only at the age of
eleven when a second communication from Jones hit
the mat.

This letter regretted Tod's failure to reply to the
first and advised him that he should make an appointment with Jones at his earliest convenience. There
seemed little point in taking the time to reply. He
had been absent from his job for three days without
leave and the slowly-filling pages of A4 were revealing him to be innocent of everything. In all his life
he had never done anything wrong.

That, however, was about to change. He put on
his coat, left the house and walked to the station
where he inquired of the fastest train to Stalemate.
Evidently Jones knew him better than he did himself.
The only way out was to confront Jones and, if
necessary, fling himself upon his mercy.

Once on the train he had the leisure to start wondering where he would find Jones when he got to
Stalemate. The address on the letter simply stated:
*Stalemate Blackmail Co-operative, next to the mermaid
factory*, no doubt a needful precaution but not very
much help, unless the mermaid factory turned out to
be the size of Battersea Power Station. More confused
than ever he left the train and accosted the first passer-
by to inquire where he might find the mermaid factory.

The passer-by responded with an unpleasantly
knowing smirk and asked if by any chance he was
looking for the lawyer Jones.

'The mermaid factory,' Tod replied, firmly.

'You're a stranger here, aren't you?'

'Obviously,' Tod said, 'or I wouldn't be asking for
directions.'

'Then I suspect that your true destination is not the mermaid factory but the premises next door.'

'Even so,' said Tod, entering into the spirit of the thing, 'I could hardly be expected to locate the premises next door to the factory until I found the factory itself.'

'If you're looking for Jones,' the passer-by persisted, imperturbably, 'he'll be at the pub at this time of day—at any time of day, come to that.'

'Which pub?—not that I intend to visit any particular pub since I am not looking for the lawyer Jones,' Tod replied, 'but I may find myself in need of refreshment later in the day.'

'After you've seen Jones,' said the passer-by, 'you will certainly be in need of refreshment. Your best bet is The Mugger's Arms; if not there try The Cod's Head or, at a pinch, The Frog's Legs. Don't bother with The Slug and Bottle—Jones never goes near the place. The beer's terrible.'

'I am not looking for Jones. Who is Jones?' Tod protested, but the passer-by had sauntered on, pausing only to pluck from a wayside bush a spray of dead man's credit card, which he stuck in his buttonhole.

Tod turned resolutely in the direction indicated by the passer-by, and pressed on up the hill, crying at intervals, 'I have never heard of the lawyer Jones!' for the benefit of anyone who might be listening. Had he once stopped to look over his shoulder he would have seen that the passer-by had halted and was making rapid jottings in a small newt-skin notebook. How was Tod to know that in his innocence he had been in conversation with Zoot Humus—but more of him later.

The first pub that he came to was The Cod's Head. The interior was dark and smoky, but as soon as he put his head round the door a chorus of voices from the gloom shouted, 'Jones isn't here!'

'Why, who is Jones?' asked Tod who was learning fast, but not fast enough.

'He was here half an hour ago,' said a youth at the bar, 'and he said he'd look in again later. But for now I should try The Mugger's Arms.'

'I'll take a pint of your finest shandy,' said Tod, and seated himself on a bar stool.

'You'll need more than a pint if you're waiting for Jones – '

'I am not waiting for Jones.'

'—he's not likely to be back before two,' the bartender said.

'Why does everyone think I am looking for the lawyer Jones?'

'How do you know he's a lawyer if you don't know who he is?' the bartender asked, shoving a foaming glass across the counter.

Tod gave up and took his pint to a dark corner, brazening out the scowls of the bartender and the looks both curious and amused that were cast in his direction by the other customers. He made his pint of shandy last two and three-quarter hours, refusing to purchase even a packet of crisps which every now and again the bartender rustled suggestively in his direction. At last the door swung open and an imposing figure swept in. Without a word, the bartender nodded towards Tod's dark corner. Tod, who had been expecting a scrawny, furtive, wall-hugging, light-shunning, hard-wringing felon of the lowest class, shrank back as the massive chap bore down upon him, extending a fat hand in greeting.

'My dear fellow, I am Jones,' he said. 'And you— no, don't tell me, you could be the next Lord Tod.'

'No, I'm not,' Tod said nervously. He had been expecting revelations, but not this particular revelation, delivered in a voice like the public address system on Liverpool Street Station.

'I didn't say you *were* Lord Tod,' Jones declaimed, 'I said you could be. Have another shandy, dear boy. Make yourself comfortable.'

'Can't we go somewhere more private?' muttered Tod, who had always assumed that blackmail was conducted behind closed doors.

'No need,' said Jones. 'Everyone knows you are here. Everyone knows that you wouldn't be here unless I had some hold over you, or was about to have.'

'You mean you haven't?'

'At the moment, no,' Jones said.

'Then why are you blackmailing me? These last few days have been hell, sheer hell. I've spent seventy-two hours trying to list every misdemeanour I have ever committed and I'm still a fortnight short of my eleventh birthday.'

'Good grief,' said Jones, 'you didn't imagine that I was going to blackmail you about something you'd already done, did you?'

'If I know you're going to blackmail me, I'm hardly likely to do it, am I?' Tod replied.

'Impetuous youth,' Jones murmured. 'You don't understand at all how these matters are conducted. Might I ask what put the idea of blackmail into your mind? I'm sure I never mentioned it.'

'Your letterhead, mainly,' Tod said.

'Is that all? Why, for all you knew I might simply be purloining office stationery for my own correspondence. I'm sure you're done something similar,' he went on, with a dreadful, complicit wink. 'Paper-clips? Wallet files?'

'You don't trick me like that,' Tod snapped. 'I've never stolen anything from the office—not from anybody.'

'An association like ours is hardly likely to waste its time blackmailing people over liberated paperclips,' Jones said, loftily. 'Ours is a grander design.'

'Then why pick on me?' Tod snarled. 'As you can see, I am scarcely qualified to be part of anyone's grand design. I am a worm, a lowly crawling thing. There are insects in the family only five generations back. Nothing you could do would bring me lower. Why me? Leave me alone.'

'Ingrate,' said Jones. 'I do not wish to bring you lower, quite the reverse, as it happens. I chose you out of thousands—well, dozens, to be accurate, and Fate took a hand. Between us we came up with you, after ransacking every telephone directory in the United Kingdom.'

'Fate?' said Tod. 'You mean you picked me out with a pin.'

'Fate picked you out with a pin,' Jones said. 'I did the donkey work. I personally spent days compiling a list of all the Tods with one "d"; far fewer of them than the other variety. It was barrel-scraping, believe me. When it was time for the pin, you happened to be underneath.'

'I see. So there's no particular reason why I should be your victim aside from the fact that I am already the victim of random selection. Don't forget,' Tod added, threateningly, 'I am not entirely unacquainted with computers.'

'Why speak of victims? So crude,' protested the deprecating Jones. 'If you accept my proposal you will be my business associate. Part of the letterhead, as you might say. We are a flourishing organization due mainly, dare I say it, to my painstaking pinwork. Another shandy? No? Then let us begin. As you may recall my saying, when first we met, you could be the next Lord Tod.'

'No,' Tod said, 'I could not. My father used to

64

boast that we were distantly connected to the Tods of Stalemate, but this was mere empty conceit. The Tod lineage is ancient. We, on the other hand, were Todd, until the final "d" was dropped by a drunken sign-writer in 1843 while painting my great-great-grandfather's name over a grog-shop doorway.'

'Let me put it to you more plainly,' said Jones. 'Read my lips. You *can* be the next Lord Tod—at no immediate cost to yourself. The last lord went to meet his maker three months ago. The search is now on for his heir. As I was his lordship's solicitor, executor and life-long friend, he entrusted me with discovering the lost claimant.'

'I am not the lost claimant,' Tod said.

'Of course you're not,' said Jones. 'The lost claimant, who has only recently become lost, I might add, is enjoying the peace that passeth all understanding not far from where we are sitting. Whatever else he is, or may become, he will never be Lord Tod, so why shouldn't you be?'

'Why should I be?' Tod said, suspiciously. 'What's in it for you? What's in it for me, come to that?'

'For you . . . well, I cannot promise you untold riches but I can offer you a fine manor house, walled garden, southern aspect, devoted domestic staff, a small dairy farm and a laboratory in which you would,' said Jones, 'be free to conduct any experiment you liked.'

'And what about you?'

'This is where we become associates,' Jones said. 'If you decide to inherit I shall, after a decent interval of time, begin to blackmail you.'

'What for? I mean, how will you justify it?'

'Your imposture, for one thing. The possibility that you murdered the lost claimant – '

'I take it that actually *you* murdered him,' Tod said.

'You don't expect me to admit that, do you? However, I can't deny that I should be in possession of certain facts that would enable me to lead Zoot Humus straight to the body. However, if you continued to pay me the agreed sum, the body would remain undisturbed.'

'Why didn't you just let the poor devil inherit what was legally his?' said Tod.

'There's not a great deal of profit in behaving legally, even for a lawyer,' said Jones.

'And in any case, how could you possibly pass me off as the rightful heir?'

Jones opened his briefcase. 'I have here,' he said, 'an exquisitely wrought family tree showing the lineage, from 1127, of the Tod family. They were never a very impressive bunch but, believe me, they were durable. Some family trees are scarcely more than bushes. On the topmost branch is a blank space. Tell me, why should your name not fill it?'

Tod, aware that most family trees are depicted as growing downwards, leaned over to look and saw that this one was indeed a tree, minutely detailed with tasteful embellishments of scroll-work and gold leaf. At the very top was a vacant twig.

'A thing of beauty, don't you think?' Jones said.

'Heart-stopping,' Tod agreed, 'but why is it tattooed on a Dover sole?'

'Since both Church and State have ceased to be patrons of the Arts, it has fallen upon the Law to fulfil that function,' Jones replied.

'Glad to hear it,' said Tod who was, in his way, also an artist. 'But I must say that I've never considered deep-sea fishing to be one of the Fine Arts.'

'You have a lot to learn about Stalemate,' Jones remarked, 'and if you decide to inherit you will, no doubt, learn it. Now, tell me, how can you resist? This document proves beyond all reasonable and unreasonable argument that whoever occupies that slot on the topmost branch is the natural and legal heir to the late Lord Tod. No one could dispute your claim. There it is in black and white and gold leaf; you are the son of Edward Tod, son of Albert Tod, son of William Tod himself brother of George Tod who begat Ernest Tod who begat Godfrey Tod, late Lord of the Manor of Stalemate who died childless or rather, who appears to have become childless since his demise.'

'It's all very well on pap—on fish,' Tod said, 'but in practice it could present problems. Supposing someone comes up to me and says "How's your father – ?" '

'Simply say that he is dead,' said Jones. 'You will have ample time to invent suitable ends for all your ancestors. I can promise you that once you have inherited you will not be troubled by a single, solitary forebear.'

'Death isn't the answer to everything,' Tod said.

'I think you'll find that it is,' said Jones.

They sat in silence. It was almost three o'clock, the cavernous bar of The Cod's Head was empty save for the bartender who lounged behind the pumps playing tunes on his teeth with a small brass-headed mallet apparently designed expressly for that purpose, and a figure seated in a corner even more shadowy than the one occupied by Tod and Jones.

'All very well,' Tod said at last, 'but as I asked you before, what's in it for you, apart from the money?'

'Primarily,' said Jones, 'my pleasure in your constant terror that I may denounce you at any moment. In spite of appearances I am a deeply religious man, godly, you might say, and as such derive enormous satisfaction from knowing that people spend their lives in daily dread that things will eventually turn out even worse than they are already. As to the financial side of things. I have calculated that your inheritance will permit you, if you handle it wisely, to pay me, on a monthly basis, one seventh of your income without missing it. It all depends on how badly you want to be Lord Tod. I will leave you to consider it. Don't hurry yourself; these things take time, I know. When you have made up your mind, well, you know where to find me.'

'Next to the mermaid factory. See here,' said Tod, 'what's to stop me going straight out of here and exposing you?'

'How?' Jones said, rising. 'At the first hint of outside intervention the evidence will be grilled and served with new potatoes and a mixed salad.'

'Are you referring to the lost claimant?' Tod asked.

'To the Dover sole, actually,' said Jones, 'but now that you mention it . . .' Moving astonishingly lightly for one of his bulk he left the alcove and passed out of the bar, pausing only to nod farewell to the bartender who was now essaying the viola part of Schubert's *Trout Quintet* on his upper and lower incisors. Almost immediately the shadowy figure in the opposite alcove rose to his feet and followed, casting a meaning leer at the bartender who flung down his mallet, sprang from behind the bar and ran to open the door, exclaiming as he did so, with a deferential bow, 'Always a pleasure to serve you, Mr Humus.'

Tod sat in his corner a while longer. Rain fell outside and the shadows deepened. From under the counter the bartender produced a tuning fork and proceeded to bring his molars up to concert pitch. Tod found the plangent trickle of notes consoling and he began to compose his thoughts. He considered his current situation. He lived in a small noisy flat overlooking a derelict canal basin. He loathed his job and, after his unexplained absence, had almost certainly lost it. He had an overdraft of three hundred pounds at the bank and no prospects. Could he give up all this in exchange for a lifetime of fear, uncertainty and deceit? There was no choice, really. Money, he said to himself, may not buy happiness but it makes unhappiness a sight more endurable. Why live wretchedly in poverty when he could live wretchedly in comfort?

'What you are doing,' said the weasel voice of his conscience, 'is tantamount to selling your soul.'

'And who wouldn't?' said Tod, bitterly.

The bartender, having tuned his teeth to his satisfaction, commenced a cascade of arpeggios which fell upon Tod's ears like the tears of angels.

'I'll give you a fiver if you'll play *Layla*,' he yelled.

'I don't do rock,' said the bartender sulkily, and plunged into Bach's *Toccata and Fugue* in D which, judging by the quality of the bass notes, involved wisdom teeth.

Back at his flat that evening Tod found himself on his doormat ankle-deep in brown envelopes, mainly containing final demands, and he realized that had he persisted with his life story he would have been able to put debt upon his so-far non-existent list of misdemeanours. Indeed, now he came to think about it, it had been impressed upon him, from his earliest years, that poverty itself was a serious crime against the State, indicative of low intelligence, low morals, poor initiative and lack of a job, this last confirmed by the brown envelope that lay on top of the heap. It was from his boss, terminating his employment.

Tod propped the letter against the coffee pot and sat contemplating it for many hours. To his ears, like an evil symphony, came heavy thumps as his neighbours kicked each other up and down stairs, the merry shouts of children pushing their friends into the canal basin, the whine of his landlord's Black and Decker as he drilled holes in the walls the better to monitor his tenants, the brisk footsteps of burglars, like mice in the skirting boards. At the back of his mind jangled the fiendish percussion of the bartender's teeth. A lifetime in thrall to the lawyer Jones could be no worse, he concluded at midnight, when he heard the arsonist upstairs leave by the fire escape. Next morning he posted his keys through the landlord's letter-box and went back to Stalemate in search of Jones.

The same loitering passer-by happened to be in the vicinity. Tod, recognizing him as the shadowy figure in The Cod's Head, and remembering his name, approached him boldly.

'Good morning, Mr Humus. Kindly direct me to the mermaid factory. It still lacks forty minutes to opening time,' he added, seeing that Humus was on the verge of argument.

Humus shrugged, tore a page from the newt-skin jotter and sketched a map.

'I take it we shall be seeing a lot more of you in future, Lord Tod,' he said.

'I doubt very much if *you* will be seeing me at all,' Tod said, and turned on his heel. Humus struck him as knowing a sight too much while there was yet scarcely anything to know.

The mermaid factory, when he reached it, was easily identified by its rusting pipework and stacks of carboys in the yard. The pipes belched and gurgled. As he passed by Tod heard faint splashings and wallowings from the interior, and the thud of a distant pump. Nor was there any doubt about the premises next door. A converted bicycle shop, with a wheel still suspended from a bracket over the porch, it now housed a number of small businesses advertised on brass plates by the front door:

THE GREAT TROCHANTER: ILLUSIONIST

STALEMATE BLACKMAIL CO-OPERATIVE
HON SEC: FIG JONES

The door stood open and as Tod stepped inside a wizened receptionist appeared at his elbow, mopping and mowing and mumbling, 'Please to come this way, Lord Tod.'

Then ahead of him the light was blocked by the gross silhouette of the lawyer Jones, proffering upon a silver salver the Dover sole, and as he thrust it fragrantly under Tod's nose, Tod saw that the vacant space at the top of the family tree was now filled by the words *Sainsbury Tod*.

'How did you know I would agree?' he faltered.

'I knew,' said Jones, 'and even had I been wrong it would not have been beyond our powers to appoint a second Sainsbury Tod. That would have been a poor look-out for you, of course. Now, there is a document or two requiring your signature – '

'Promising to make over to you one seventh of my income – '

'You do not seriously imagine that *that* is going to appear in print, do you?' Jones said. 'Business of this kind is conducted upon a handshake;' and his powerful mauler wrapped itself around Tod's hand. 'I was known as "Strangler" Fig Jones at the Varsity,' the lawyer murmured.

The documents signed, Jones conducted the new Lord Tod to his manor house, making only two diversions on the way; one to The Cod's Head, for obvious reasons, one to a corner of a certain plot of land, to view a certain grave.

'The lost claimant?' inquired Tod, with a shudder.

'Certainly not,' said Jones, indicating a modest hump in the grass. 'This is the late Lord Tod; the lost claimant is still lost. The headstone has yet to be erected—you'll be seeing to that. What an historic moment; the late Lord Tod and the latest Lord Tod. Remind me to give you the name of a good monumental mason.'

— 6 —
Death by Soap

When I woke up on Saturday morning I knew at once that the dreaded west wind had struck. The roar of a spring gale was punctuated by the snap, crackle and pop of washing filled with air and when I looked out of the window I saw Gwen Cattermole's red duvet cover, king-sized, of course, swelling over the fence as though a sky-diver's parachute was landing on our lawn. Twelve white nappies, like a skein of kites, streamed along the line beside it. There would be hard words spoken at breakfast.

The wind that blew down Coldharbour had already passed over Old Compton. I wondered if the same exciting scenes were taking place in the Crossleys' garden. I thought of them all, Mrs Crossley at the line with pegs between her teeth, Paul in his tent, Mr Crossley sawing up the staircase, and Elaine; what was Elaine doing?

What I wanted to do was rush out of the house, head into the wind and go straight down to Old Compton, to find Elaine and pick up the saga of Stalemate where we had left off. Why exactly did Lord Tod collect corpses and what experiments was he going to conduct in his laboratory? What was the truth about Zoot Humus? What went on in the mermaid factory? What did Captain Cheeseheart do with the souls his hound brought home?

Instead I stayed in bed. Perhaps I ought to ring Elaine first and find out what her plans were. Some families had ancient rituals for weekends. We had been like that once, in Stoke Newington. On Saturday mornings we all got into the car and went to do a Big Shop at the supermarket. Then we had lunch together, outside at The Black Prince in summer, McDonald's in winter. In the afternoon Dad watched sport on telly and I went out with friends and in the evening we'd go to the cinema or get a take-away and a video. I didn't know if all this had stopped because I was getting older or because we lived in Compton Rosehay. In a way I missed it but I didn't want it back again. I wanted something else, but I didn't know what.

I still stayed in bed. Perhaps I shouldn't ring Elaine, shouldn't rush things. I was remembering when I first went out with Peter Rafferty, and Mark Willows before that, remembering that feeling of wanting to be with them all the time and letting it happen, or making it happen and then discovering that in almost no time we had used up everything we felt about each other. We would have used it up anyway, but with a bit of caution we could have made it last longer.

Perhaps Elaine didn't want to see me as much as I wanted to see her. Not that I felt the same way about Elaine as I did about Peter and Mark, I just wanted to be with the Crossleys again, among people who made me feel happy instead of wary. But the Crossleys had each other. Elaine did not need anyone else, she never got bored with her own company. Perhaps Stalemate was not meant to last; it was a one-off joke that would sicken and die if we tried to make it last.

I must not rush things. Instead of going down to Old Compton or ringing Elaine I did what I usually did on Saturday mornings and walked to Manor Garth to poke around the shops and run into friends, sit in Jangles and discuss what was happening in all the soaps and, if Rowena came in, cellulite. But that day I did not run into friends and when I passed

Jangles I saw the sign for Zen yoghurt. After that I found I was actively taking steps to avoid friends and when I saw Lynzi and Marie approaching down The Cloister I doubled back and went into Sainsbury's and wandered round for twenty minutes with an empty basket until I must have had every security camera in the place trained on me. I looked for Lord Tod and tried to imagine that where racks of tinned vegetables and coffee jars and washing powder reared up on either side I was really surrounded by the yews and dripping elms of Stalemate Manor. But it would not work. I could not do Stalemate on my own. When I was little I could turn the back garden, the park or any street into foreign territory without even trying. Now, no matter how hard I tried, I could not conjure Stalemate into life. What Elaine had said was true; it was there but I could not see it.

In the end I put a pack of roasted peanuts in the wire basket and went through the checkout. Mum and Dad were out when I got home, but there was a message for me stuck to the television screen. We always left messages there, it was the one place that everybody would be certain to look, sooner or later.

The message was brief: *CHARLOTTE! someone called Eileen phoned. Do you want to go round? Leave a note if you go out.*

Someone called Eileen. The fact that Mum had got the name wrong seemed a kind of safeguard. If word ever reached her about the bizarre family in Old Compton the mythical Eileen would be my alibi. Elaine Crossley? Never heard of her. I don't know anyone in Old Compton.

I replaced the message with the requested note and ran out of the house, leaving it empty save for the shadows of Mrs Cattermole's washing, now filling our living room with a kind of phantom bouncing. Across the road a bus was drawing in to the kerb. I leapt on to it and we cruised away up Coldharbour, along Starveacre and Copsewood, pausing at Manor Garth and then on down The Glebe where Mrs McCadaver had answered the door to the first Martian missionary. As we approached the row of Anglo-Saxon cottages and I stood up to ring the bell, I saw Elaine pushing letters into the pillar box opposite the mermaid factory.

It was a functional, grimy place; by Compton Rosehay standards, filthy. Between the bicycle shop and a collapsing shed, a driveway, stained with oil, sloped down to a pair of double doors.

'O Glee . . .' Elaine said thoughtfully, looking up at the broken sign that spanned the drive.

'The rest fell off,' I said, pointing to the other half which was propped against the gateless gatepost . . . SON. WELDING, it said.

'It didn't *fall*,' Elaine said. 'Someone threw a brick and dashed it to the ground when the nuns rioted in '76.'

'It's a religious invocation,' I said, 'like "O God our help in ages past".'

The double doors at the far end of the drive stood open, to reveal a gloomy interior lit by flashes of violent light. In front of the doors stood a couple of severely damaged cars, one with a mangled bonnet and the other a crushed rear end. Beside them was parked a newly-sprayed vehicle exhibiting no sign of injury and pointing towards the road, ready to drive away.

'You know what's going on, don't you?' I said, as we walked down the concrete road to Old Compton. 'Gleeson's wicked mechanics are making new cars out of old ones, welding backs to fronts and putting them on the road with forged log books.'

'Gleeson?' Elaine said. 'Obadiah Gleet. The cars are just a blind, a red herring. He got the idea of welding car bodies together after he'd discovered how to do it with human ones.'

'He's not in cahoots with Lord Tod, is he?'

'They collaborate occasionally. Zoot Humus is still collecting evidence. Actually Gleet started out investigating Frankenstein's theories. He hoped to create a race of zombie-like creatures who would do his evil work – '

'What evil work?'

'The world is not yet prepared. But there was a limit to the number of zombies he could release into a place the size of Stalemate. People would notice— even in Compton Rosehay. Look, there goes one now. Anyway, after he'd perfected the method he diversified into mermaids.'

'Does everyone know that it's a mermaid factory?'

'Naturally. It's the main employer locally, which is why the authorities have never closed it down even though the toxic fumes from the tanks are known to cause leukaemia and genetic deformities, and people whose houses back on to it keep complaining about the loud splashing at midnight.'

'I know Professor Scrapie wrote to the *Times*, but then he complains about everything,' I said.

'Zoot Humus would never have got on to George Clyster if the Professor hadn't written to the *Times* about the contents of Mrs Clyster III's dustbin,' said Elaine. I walked beside her, experiencing what I could only describe as a surge of achievement. Perhaps people felt like that after having a baby. All the frustration and disappointment that had built up during the morning as I walked round Sainsbury's evaporated. Where had Professor Scrapie come from? I had spoken his name and suddenly, he was there. We both knew him. We'd always known him.

The professor, a grim Glaswegian known to his students as 'Auld Scrapie', had been appointed to the

Chair of Comparative Malacology at the University of Stalemate back in '76. Stalemate still remembered the night his slugs had broken out. Professor Scrapie had won a reputation as an international expert on Mad Slug Disease, and questions were asked in the House of Commons as the professor's crazed slugs, some of them as much as 80 cm long, rampaged through Stalemate in a frenzied orgy of eating. Gateposts were gnawed down to the roots. Captain Cheeseheart went on record as saying, 'Man, you don't know what fear is until you've looked into the eyes of a deranged slug.'

None of this, or his subsequent reputation as a public nuisance, had stopped the professor from complaining to everyone about everything. I asked how he had fared over Obadiah Gleet and the mermaid factory, since Elaine clearly knew more about this enterprise than I did.

'Well, the Public Health Inspector had to go round,' Elaine said, 'but Gleet persuaded him that his giant tanks were simply a means of storing rain-water which, owing to his erupting skin condition, he needed for thrice-nightly baths. And the liquid in them was so cloudy (natural algae, according to Gleet) that the PHI couldn't see the mermaids forming.'

'*Forming*? What was he doing, then? Creating them by electrolysis out of a kind of primaeval soup? Where does the welding come in?'

'You don't imagine he was welding protoplasm? Get real. It was just the principle of two into one that attracted him to car-nobbling. What you've got to remember is the basic design concept of the mermaid: front end human, back end fish; known to scientists as *homo ichthyanthropos*. Sailors have been faking them for years, but Gleet was no faker. His mermaids were for real.'

'He was breeding them?'

'He was *not* breeding them. He was almost certainly getting the human ends from Lord Tod – '

'What happened to the rest of the bodies?'

'Remember the mass trouser famine of '76?' Elaine said, cryptically. 'The other end was the result of an arrangement between Gleet and Dagobert the poet and fishmonger. In his tanks Gleet was concocting a broth of all know factors for the creation of human life – '

'So it *was* primaeval soup!'

'—into which he introduced his mermaid components, lightly clamped together. At a constant temperature of 33.7° Celsius, the two halves began to conjoin.'

'How did they breathe?'

'They were amphibious; like tadpoles to begin with. Gills formed in the neck.'

'How?'

'Some property of the primaeval soup. But as soon as the two halves became whole, the mermaids put their heads above water and breathed air. Gleet had to put little seats in the tanks. Mind you, this didn't happen all at once. Night after night, by the sullen glare of 15 watt bulbs, he sat watching the tanks, regulating the controls of the heating system to keep the temperature steady, monitoring heart beats. In the tanks the great sluggish forms flexed and twisted, obscured by the murk but occasionally scraping a fin against the glass. Passers-by described it as the sound of a giant fingernail on a slate.'

'That,' I said, with a burst of inspiration, 'was what kept Professor Scrapie awake at nights – '

Two afflictions could be guaranteed to goad Professor Scrapie into action. One he referred to archly as back trouble, which regularly attacked him at

10.30 in the evening when the night shift came on at the mermaid factory, at the end of his garden.

'Trouble *at* the back, heh, heh,' said the professor, before sitting down to write to the *Times*.

The other complaint was throat trouble. It was throat trouble today. Next door Mrs Gnarlene Throat was adopting another pathetic little delinquent in addition to the eleven who were already crammed into the house on Copsewood, although it was rare for more than three or four ever to appear at the same time. Some were orphans; only three were definitely known to be the natural offspring of Mrs Throat although, of course, they were by her three previous husbands and were called Josephine Cramp, Kevin Twitch and Wayne Spasm. In fact, Gnarlene Throat had still been Mrs Spasm on the day that God created Stalemate, but Len Spasm, running to save little Kevin's pet wombat from being attacked by one of the professor's slugs, had fallen fatally beneath the treads of a half-track driven by Reverend Mother Maria de los Angeles on an errand of mercy. (The professor certainly thought it was an errand of mercy as he helped to pick Len out of the treads.) Gnarlene hated to talk about death. 'He was written out,' she would tell people, coyly.

Sophie, Kylie and Marsha Throat had become instant sisters when adopted by Gnarlene not three weeks after marrying Stan Throat. Gnarlene had immediately become eight months pregnant and given birth four weeks prematurely although the baby, little Gayle, registered on a pre-dated birth certificate, had not been seen since the christening.

Throat babies had exactly a fortnight to establish themselves; after that they were packed away until it was time to go to school. If they were lucky they might attain school age in a matter of months although the rigours of this accelerated growth programme often had startling effects upon the children; blue-eyed blonds mutated into brown-eyed brunettes and little Kevin had undergone a radical sex-change having been christened Tammy-Anne. Other assorted fosterlings *chez* Throat were Craig Crass and Bobby Gross whose parents, all four, were mad, bad and dangerous to know and who reappeared at intervals to lure them away from Gnarlene's loving arms; Junie and Joanie Blurt, the abandoned twins— so abandoned that even the social services had backed off—and little Duggie who had been up in the bathroom for three years, maturing.

Now, today, Josie, Junie and Joanie had come home with Kathleen-Mavourneen Shape whose mother, although none of them knew it, was about to be written out in an airline disaster. Kathleen-Mavourneen was a wild child, heavily made up, with a ring through her nose—no decorative gem winking seductively in one nostril but an iron hoop that she'd nicked from a stud bull, driven through the gristly bit in the middle. Kathleen-Mavourneen had made the hole herself with a red-hot kebab skewer. She wore eighteen-hole DMs and had a poacher's pocket in her school blazer where she kept her stash. As Gnarlene welcomed her to the family her glossy carmine lips drooped in a sultry pout, and her kohl-rimmed eyes played speculatively over Kevin Twitch, Craig and Bobby. Craig and Bobby had come ready-made at fifteen and sixteen respectively. Kevin had simply grown up very fast; primary school one day, GCSE the next.

'Kathleen-Mavourneen can go two ways,' Elaine said. 'Time will tell. Either she'll turn out as raunchy as she looks, create havoc and lust among Bobby, Craig and Kevin – '
    'What about Wayne?'

'He left home to find himself; caught the bus at the end of the road. You know what happens to people who catch the bus at the end of the road. Either she'll create havoc among Bobby, Craig and Kevin, and sibling rivalry among Josie, Junie, Joanie, Sophie, Kylie and Marsha, or Gnarlene's patent sugar solution will strip away the make-up to reveal the scared little girl she really is. Then she'll abandon her stash, rip the ring out of her nose and go back to school to do her A levels.'

'She's only thirteen.'

'She'll grow up quickly. She's a Throat, isn't she?'

'Only a quasi-Throat.'

' "A Throat's a Throat, for a' that," as Professor Scrapie would say.'

'She's still a Shape. She won't be a Throat until Gnarlene adopts her. You know what Shapes are like.'

We had not, up to that moment, given any thought to what the Shapes were like, but it was not going to take long to find out. There was a house near the end of Mockbeggar which hung its curtains back to front, with the pattern and pelmet facing the street.

'Empty show,' Elaine had said, when I pointed it out to her the previous evening while we had still been high on Zen yoghurt. 'Obsessed with what the neighbours think. They clean the mortar round the bricks with a toothbrush every morning, before it gets light. Even the cat has to be oiled before they let it out.' We had named the house 'Posturings'.

'Kathleen-Mavourneen doesn't live at Posturings, does she?' Elaine said.

'Where else?' I said. 'And how could they keep her there, looking the way she does? There were endless rows. It was all right while Kathleen-Mavourneen was little. Her mother, Mrs Deirdre Shape, would dress her in pink frocks and white socks with lace round the ankles and those dinky patent leather shoes with sling backs and wedge heels especially designed for growing feet.'

'Big shiny ribbons in her hair.'

'Naturally. She had a chignon at eighteen months old. That made it easier to polish her forehead.'

'She must have been blonde.'

'Like corn silk. Mrs Deirdre Shape would have preferred easy-care viscose, but you can't have everything. Then the trouble started. Kathleen-Mavourneen got into bad company—one of the McCadavers.'

'I thought they were eminently respectable,' said Elaine, who was largely responsible for the McCadavers.

'Not this branch of the family. They came from the wrong side of the tracks. The Stalemate Development Corporation laid down special tracks to keep them on the wrong side of. That's how the railway came to Stalemate.'

'This lot go in for multiple births,' Elaine said, regaining control of the McCadavers. 'All nine McCadavers are either eleven or fifteen. Lydia McCadaver exerted an evil influence over Kathleen-Mavourneen. In fact it was Lydia Mac who persuaded Kathleen-Mavourneen to dye her hair black. Who took her to Dagobert, the fishmonger poet – '

'Who has a tattoo parlour in his back premises – '

'Of course. That accounts for the strange case of the Illuminated Turbot, which Zoot Humus will solve in due course.'

'Has this anything to do with Lord Tod's family tree?'

'Peripherally. Think Dagobert, think fish.'

'Kathleen-Mavourneen had *Hygiene stinks* tattooed across her shoulders. Then Lydia persuaded her to have her nose pierced. By this time Mrs Deirdre

Shape was beginning to notice a change in her little girl.'

'What about Mr Shape?' Elaine said.

'He is of no account. A sweeper-up at the mermaid factory. Deirdre has confined him to the garden shed since the day he brought in mud on the soles of his boots. Deirdre believes that mud *breeds* spontaneously and brings forth silverfish.'

'The neighbourhood was roused day and night by Deirdre and Kathleen-Mavourneen screaming at each other – '

'Deirdre's *refined* scream is in the sound archives at the BBC. They use it a lot in radio drama because no living actress can equal the decibel rate.'

'Unfortunately, Deirdre's refined scream was exactly the same resonant frequency as the bell at the convent of the Combat Sisters.'

'Wait a minute—who *are* the Combat Sisters?'

'We'll find out. This resonant frequency was also shared by Sister Orthodontia's wooden leg.'

Reverend Mother Maria de los Angeles was sorely tried by the inexplicable tolling of the bell when no one was around to ring it. The more impressionable nuns thought that it must be the ghost of Sister Acts who hanged herself from the bell rope but Sister Orthodontia herself blamed the gradual disintegration of her prosthesis on an infestation of death-watch beetle. They called in Zoot Humus who collected data. The first conclusion he came to was that the tolling of the bell always coincided with a fresh fall of sawdust. Zoot walked round Stalemate for six weeks with a tuning fork until, one night, when all was still, Zoot found himself at a point on a direct line between the convent and Posturings. On his left, Deirdre's refined scream pierced the limpid air, on his right the great convent bell, known as Old Nick, after Nicholas Sanies who cast it, commenced tolling. Zoot Humus held aloft his tuning fork. With a melodious twang it began to hum. Unknown to Zoot, at that same moment Sister Orthodontia's wooden leg fell away entirely to dust.

Apprised of the phenomenon, Reverend Mother Maria de los Angeles went round to Posturings to remonstrate with Deirdre, but Deirdre was obdurate. So long as Kathleen-Mavourneen pursued her path to ruin, Deirdre would just have to go on screaming at her.

'What would you expect a concerned parent to do?' Deirdre wanted to know.

'Perhaps try screaming on a different frequency,' Reverend Mother suggested.

'This is my *daughter* we're talking about here,' said Deirdre, her voice beginning to rise.

'No, it's your scream,' said Reverend Mother Maria de los Angeles. 'Your daughter left home three weeks ago and has been living rough ever since. If you'd stopped screaming for five minutes you might have noticed that.'

But Deirdre only screamed the louder. The bell tolled incessantly, and a tank cracked at the mermaid factory. Professor Scrapie, needless to say, was writing to the *Times*.

Cue for the Throats to step in. Josie Cramp and Junie and Joanie Blurt knew that if Gnarlene was told about misguided Kathleen-Mavourneen Shape, her motherly heart would ache to draw her into the warm, not to say humid, family circle of the Throats.

'Well, sweethearts,' said Gnarlene, 'we'll have to ask Stan what he thinks. After all, this is his home too, now, chooks.'

'Ow, Gnarlene, we'll have a family council and vote on it, won't we?' cried little Duggie who had finally broken out of the bathroom and fought his way downstairs in time for his sixth birthday.

'Why do we have to ask Stan?' demanded Junie and Joanie. 'He'll only say, "It's your decision, sweetheart," and we'll be back where we started.'

'He's been holding negotiations with his script writer,' said Gnarlene. 'Now he's got equal decision-making rights written into his contract. Oh, hark, the baby's crying, Josie. Go and see to her, there's a love.'

'Which baby?' said Josie, understandably confused.

Gnarlene did a quick calculation on her fingers. 'It must be little Gayle.'

'*I'm* little Gayle,' said a hoarse-voiced redhead of thirteen, pushing her way into the kitchen.

'This house won't seem the same without a baby in it,' complained Sophie.

'Well, that was what I wanted to speak to you about,' said Gnarlene. 'Stan and I have something to tell you, haven't we, Stan?'

'Too right,' said Stan, struggling out from the cupboard under the stairs where he had spent the last fortnight, looking for a light bulb.

'Who's that?' said Marsha, running to Gnarlene with a little cry of fear.

'Why, that's your stepfather, sweetheart,' Gnarlene said.

'I've never seen him before in my life!' Marsha shrieked.

'You must have been out shopping when we got married,' Stan said. Suddenly a voice by the fridge called out, 'Dad!'

'You talking to me?' Stan said. 'Do I know you?'

'Nah, not you.' It was Craig Crass who had spoken. His eyes were fixed with wild surmise upon a rugged figure who filled the doorway. 'Dad, what are you doing here?'

'Just bust out of the slammer and came over to see my kids,' said the stranger, huskily. 'God, Craig, you've turned into a son to be proud of. Who's your mother?'

At that moment Wayne Spasm rushed in, waving a newspaper. 'Oh, Jeez,' he sobbed, 'I don't know how to tell you. Gayle, Joanie, Bobby, Kylie and little Duggie have all been killed when a Boeing 747 struck an iceberg. Your mum's croaked too,' he added, seeing that Kathleen-Mavourneen was standing at his elbow. Suddenly the kitchen seemed strangely empty.

'What in heck's going on?' Stan demanded. 'Seems like only a minute ago and they were all standing round us, one big happy family . . .'

'If you ask me, two pages have got stuck together,' Wayne grunted. 'I thought I was in Vancouver. I should get along over to the hospital if I were you, Stan. You're going to die of your injuries. Sorry.'

'It was a sad ten minutes for the Throats,' I said.

'It was a field day for Lord Tod,' said Elaine.

'Why *does* he collect corpses?'

'Be patient. Zoot Humus will reveal all in his own good time.'

'When he's solved the mystery of the Illuminated Turbot. Remember, he is the sole representative of law and order in Stalemate.'

'What about the lawyer Jones?'

'From what I recall about the lawyer Jones,' I said, 'he is not exactly conducive to law and order.'

'Oh, don't be such a prig,' said Elaine. 'You know what they say: Justice doesn't need to be done, it only needs to be seen.'

— 7 —
Dagobert's Adventures in the Retail Trade

Easter was late that year, and on the last day of term Elaine and I decided by lunch-time that to stay for another three and a half hours till the end of the afternoon would be over and above the call of duty. Stalemate was waiting and we had discovered, very quickly, that it was unwise to do Stalemate in school. Accordingly, when Red Alert sounded at the end of the morning, we headed for Manor Garth, making a detour through the bosky brickwork of Herdsman's Close. We intended to go to the library and then spend the afternoon in Jangles Coffee House, perhaps investigating the after-effects of Zen yoghurt, but there was, *en route*, a house at the end of Herdsman's Close that we were keeping under observation.

The Close was not a close at all, you could get in on foot from either end, and where it emerged into Copsewood the last house was set at an angle to the rest so that its front windows faced Copsewood itself. This, as I explained to Elaine, was to give the impression that many centuries ago the original herdsman's goat had made a skittish side-step round a tussock of grass and that the Close had slavishly followed its track.

What interested us about this house was its entry-phone. There were entry-phones in the doorways to the flats above the shops in Manor Garth, which was understandable since the flats were at least one, sometimes three flights up, but the house in Herdsman's Close was just a house, with identical curtains at the upstairs and downstairs windows, so we knew that it was not divided into flats. No one expected the entry-phone. When we saw people going up the front path they always knocked, or pressed the illuminated button that activated tubular bells. Finally, getting no answer, they would look around and see the entry-phone. That was never answered either. Although we had taken to passing the house daily and, lately, two or three times daily, we never saw anyone go in or come out.

'I don't think it's a house,' Elaine said. 'It's a premises.'

'Like the mermaid factory?'

'Possibly, but not so obvious. The mermaid factory is overtly a factory. This place is passing itself off as something else. Whoever lives there does not wish to advertise his or her activities.'

'It couldn't be Zoot Humus, could it?'

'No, he's at the bicycle shop.'

'He doesn't *live* at the bicycle shop.'

'But he only sees clients there. No one would visit his home. No one would dare to visit his home.'

We were approaching the house, now. A woman who had been standing on the doorstep came down the path, crossed over Copsewood and stood gazing up at the first floor windows, apparently looking for signs of life. As usual, there was none.

'Extraordinary, isn't it?' Elaine said. 'For people who are never at home, they get an incredible number of visitors.'

'Maybe they are at home,' I said. 'Maybe they spend their entire lives in hiding and come out only at night. Could it be another branch of the McCadavers?'

'Too many of *them*. They couldn't hope to remain undetected, especially since Nigel's disastrous experimental theatre venture in '76.'

'Exiled royalty, perhaps, awaiting the secret signal for insurrection.'

We knew that exiled royalty hung out somewhere in Stalemate, waiting for their network of supporters to overthrow the House of Windsor, what time they would sally forth triumphantly and claim the throne that had been withheld from them for five hundred years. We had thought at first that they must be Middle-European princelings with a tenuous claim on the English crown, but they turned out to be the Plantagenets. Richard III had not, after all, died at the Battle of Bosworth in 1485 but, hideously injured, had been spirited away by faithful followers and had last been spotted working in a supermarket in Reading.

As we passed the house the woman crossed back again, strode resolutely up the front path and pressed the buzzer on the entry-phone. Simultaneously we stopped, loitered and were rewarded. The entry-phone had replied! The woman on the doorstep spoke into the grille and to our astonishment, the door clicked open.

'Did you see that?' Elaine said. 'Someone's got in at last.'

'She must have known the code.'

'The code! Why didn't we think of it before?'

'You know who lives there?'

'We should have known from the start; Dagobert the fishmonger poet!'

By the time we had got to Jangles and ordered our Zen yoghurt we had worked out that only the initiated knew that Dagobert's premises were a shop, and that admittance was gained by a system of coded signals via the entry-phone. Fellow poets, after identifying themselves, had to compose and recite, within three minutes, a haiku on any subject that Dagobert cared to name. The subjects were always related to fish and Dagobert was compiling an anthology of doorstep haiku. Customers wanting to be tattooed had to beat a complex rhythm on the door in a time signature nominated by Dagobert. People who simply wished to purchase fish had, after stating their requirements, to cross to the far side of the road and sing Dagobert's fish song, substituting the item of their choice in the lines:

'Bliss was it in that dawn to be alive,
But to be a fish was very heaven.'

'What do the uninitiated make of these performances?' I said. 'What do they *think* goes on in there?'

'I'll tell you what they *don't* think,' Elaine said, 'they don't for one moment imagine that Dagobert is a poet *and* a fishmonger *and* a tattooist. In fact, the only person who even suspects is Zoot Humus – '

'Ah; the strange case of the Illuminated Turbot.'

'I don't think you realize,' Elaine said, 'that the whole thing developed from Dagobert's failure to get his poetry published by conventional means . . .'

Back in '76 the University Press printed, in an edition of five hundred, his first collection, *Mollusc*, and sold fifteen copies, mainly to Dagobert's relatives, many of whom died after reading it, not that there was any obvious connection. Although disheartened, Dagobert remained, nevertheless, convinced that his poetry was worth reading, even at the cost of human life, and for some months staggered along on Social Security, flogging remaindered copies at a reduced price on street corners. Then Fortune smiled on him twice in one week. First it turned out that his late cousin had, in his will, bequeathed to Dagobert the residue of his last business venture; fifteen cases of prime Hungarian kippers. This did not seem, at first, an unqualified blessing. Dagobert panicked and started handing out free kippers with every book sold, but time was passing. The kippers were ripening. Not only were people refusing to buy Dago-bert's poetry, they were crossing the street to avoid the kippers.

Then Fortune smiled again. His auntie was called to meet her maker and left to Dagobert her house and the tools of her trade; needles, pigments, pattern books . . . Dagobert had never thought of becoming a tattooist or a fishmonger, but the combination of the kippers and the needles seemed to him more than simple coincidence. He realized that Destiny had merely been biding its time, testing his resolve, his moral fibre, waiting to see if he would prove worthy of Divine Intervention. He had. His future was sud-denly revealed.

It was not all plain sailing, however. What Dago-bert had never understood was that the Anti-Poets were behind the failure of his book. He had assumed that it was the result of public indifference to poetry in general and his in particular and he was right, but the public's indifference was generated by over-whelming waves of negative thoughts emanating from the Anti-Poets at their mass-meditation ses-sions, which were disguised as party conferences. And things were not improving. He finally realized that someone or something was blocking his poetry. The Anti-Poets were out to get him.

It took him some while to work out what was going on. Although he was gaining a reputation for the quality and texture of his tattoos, and the fish trade was booming, Dagobert was still brooding over his failure to find a publisher for his poetry. One of the facilities he offered in the tattoo parlour was a tasteful cartouche framing one of his sonnets. Plenty of the customers opted for the cartouche but few had the patience or inclination to remain stationary while Dagobert composed and inscribed the sonnet. His dream, which he confided to Zoot Humus after the case of the Illuminated Turbot was solved, was to tattoo an entire five-act verse drama on a great white shark. Most people simply wanted *Mum* or *I love Sonia* in their cartouche. A passing able-seaman survived the first line of Dagobert's sonnet to his mistress's armpit and then died of boredom.

'Force 15 on the Auger scale.'

'The what?'

'The international scale of tedium—named after Mr Auger, the most boring man in the world.'

'Couldn't Dagobert finish tattooing the corpse to his satisfaction?'

'Lord Tod . . .'

'Of course. Round like a flash.'

'How did Dagobert identity the Anti-Poets?'

'By the codes, naturally. Anti-Poets ain't got rhythm. They can't beat tattoos on the door, they do not respond to Dagobert's fish song and, the biggest give-away of the lot, they cannot compose haiku in three minutes, or even three hours. No Anti-Poet crossed Dagobert's doorstep.'

'Except once – '

'The strange case of the Illuminated Turbot.'

'It was the single incursion of an Anti-Poet into Dagobert's premises that gave Zoot any hint that there was a case to be solved.'

'Of course, the turbot—the ultimate blunt instrument!'

All this was yet to transpire. Meanwhile, Dagobert was on the verge of self-destructing with frustration; and then he had his great idea. From his upstairs window he had a distant but uninterrupted view of the ring road and thus was sole witness to the first apparition at the London Road Roundabout. A voice spoke to Dagobert from a cloud of blinding light:

'Embellish the fish!' At first it made no sense, but for three days he pondered it in his mind until at three o'clock one morning in the chill hours before the dawn he found himself pacing feverishly through the rooms of his premises, from study to fish counter, from fish counter to tattoo parlour. Suddenly he looked down and saw that in his wanderings he had plucked a small flounder from the fish counter and carried it into the tattoo parlour. As in a dream his hands had tattooed upon it the words, *I wandered, lonely as a fish*.

Then he understood the vision. Then he understood why Fate had been picking off his relatives in so prodigal a fashion, thus bestowing upon him the fish trade and the tattoo parlour in addition to his gift for poetry which was simply genetic. He was to tattoo the poems on the fish!

In a creative frenzy he raced to the fish counter, selected a fine plaice, laid it white side uppermost on the tattooing couch and began, there and then, to compose a sonnet. By mid-day he was finished. By five o'clock the plaice, and the poem, had been sold. After that there was no stopping him; fish sales rocketed. Without meaning to he had hit on an unrivalled marketing device. Nowhere else in the *world* could one purchase tattooed fish.

Then the Anti-Poets got wind of it.

This was a result of the actions of Professor Scrapie who was so often the innocent cause of dissent in Stalemate. Scrapie ordered a fine salmon which he served at a dinner party. Now the skin of a salmon leaves little space for tattooing, but on the pale underbelly Dagobert had inscribed a triolet. Unknown to the professor, his guest of honour, regarded by the world as a humble Member of Parliament, was a leading light among the Anti-Poets. Poring over his fillet of salmon this villain made out the following words:

> Down to the pond they race to spawn,
>   The newt, the toad, the dauntless frog.
> Unlike the solitary prawn
> Down to the pond they race to spawn.
> As frenzied lemmings in the dawn,
>   Through fire and tempest, frost and fog;
> Down to the pond they race to spawn,
>   The newt, the toad, the dauntless frog.

The title and signature had already disappeared down the respective gullets of the persons seated on his right and left, but he was in no doubt as to what he had discovered. He choked—all Anti-poets react violently to verse, particularly if it rhymes—blamed a fish bone in his throat and demanded to know where the professor had obtained the salmon. The professor told him; from Dagobert, in Copsewood. Then the Anti-Poet, lingering after the other guests had departed, plied the professor with his own strong drink and wormed from him the secret of how to gain access to Dagobert's premises.

Next morning, after meditating in a negative way, the Anti-Poet went along to Dagobert's doorstep and pressed the buzzer on the entry-phone.

'Tell me what you desire,' said Dagobert, down the line.

'Fish!' cried the Anti-Poet.

'You know what to do,' said Dagobert, and went to his window to watch the customer, as he thought, cross the road, fling wide his arms and intone:

> 'Bliss was it in that dawn to be alive,
>   But to be a carp was very heaven.'

Then Dagobert flung wide his door and the Anti-Poet sprang inside, yelling 'Gotcha!'

This was an undoubted vulgarism but he was, after all, an Anti-Poet, and nothing much rhymes with gotcha. What he had not known was that when he pressed the buzzer on the entry-phone, Dagobert was putting the finishing touches to his latest masterpiece, a sestina on the theme of fly-casting, tattooed on a turbot. Even he could recognize that he had been touched by genius as he worked, and to celebrate he had decorated the capital letter of each line with monkish illumination similar to that with which he had decorated Lord Tod's family tree for the lawyer Jones.

Interrupted by the entry-phone he was still clutch-ing the turbot by the tail. As the Anti-Poet finished the fish song he activated the catch on the front door and went down hospitably to welcome his customer and conduct him personally to the fish counter. When, instead of a bona fide carp-seeker he was con-fronted by a demented figure leaping up the steps and yelling 'Gotcha!' he realized that in spite of his precautions he was in the presence of an Anti-Poet. Without pause for thought he raised the turbot in his fist and smote the Anti-Poet over the head. In his death throes the Anti-Poet wrested the turbot from Dagobert's grip and fell backwards down the steps, lifeless.

Dagobert closed the door, cursing the loss of his turbot and his sestina, and went back to the tattoo parlour, picking up a haddock *en route*. Within minutes he was at work again. Meanwhile, out in the street, as the Anti-Poet lay stiffening at the foot of the steps, who should come snuffling round the corner but Zoot Humus.

Zoot Humus appeared to be a popular figure around the streets of Stalemate. As he strode mutter-ing along the pavements, swathed in his opera cloak and with his black fedora jammed over his eyes, the little children would run to greet him, housewives hurried to their front gates to offer him fresh-baked apple pies, hardened criminals jostled with each other to hang garlands of flowers around his neck and press small coins into his palm.

'How they love him,' strangers exclaimed. 'Behold the rewards of incorruptibility—the affection and trust of your fellow men.' But the facts were more sinister. Zoot Humus was only incorruptible North-North-West, as Hamlet might have said. Ninety-five per cent of the time he was as honest as the day is long, but now and again the mood took him, the wind changed, and then he was as corruptible as all get out.

Zoot was in the business of detection solely for his own gratification. He loved the truth, but as a miser loves gold. He had no desire to share it. Thus, if he got to the root of a problem there was no guarantee that the real perpetrator of the crime would be brought to justice. Zoot might very well lay the blame at another door entirely. The public outpourings of affection and esteem were the result of naked fear. None knew whom Zoot might take it into his head to incriminate next.

Prominent persons with whom Zoot Humus had had dealings would forgather and discuss him in muted voices.

'In your opinion,' said the lawyer Jones, to Lord Tod and Ernest Giblets, one evening in The Mugger's Arms, 'is the man a total cynic, a simple psychopath—or is there some deep and hitherto unexplained reason for his crusade against justice?'

'It hadn't occurred to me that Humus is crusading against anything,' Giblets said. 'A crusade implies an end result, a final triumph.'

'Quite,' said Lord Tod who after a short time in Stalemate had progressed from lemonade shandy to

Polish vodka. 'Humus is merely pledged to perverting the course of justice. He is dedicated to spreading alarm and despondency.'

'And yet he is, according to his lights, an honest man.'

'A rigidly honest man,' Jones chipped in.

'He never deceives himself.'

'Striding about spreading alarm and despondency and deep suspicion,' ruminated Lord Tod.

He was right. After Zoot Humus had passed along a street, everyone looked askance at the neighbours, asking themselves, 'Am I to be blamed for what *she* has done? Are they under suspicion for what *I* have done?'

Dagobert, however, lost not a moment's respose in entertaining such suspicions. By his own reckoning the death of the Anti-Poet was a necessary evil— not at all that much of an evil, either, when he came to think about it—almost a virtue, in fact. Like many a genius before him he was entirely amoral. If he'd had any kind of a guilty conscience he would have stolen out again and, if not removed the body, at least recovered the turbot. But he was not thinking along lines of incriminating evidence; he was not aware of Zoot's activities; he was barely aware of anything except fish, tattooing and poetry. Moreover, it never occurred to him that anyone in Stalemate might have opinions about him. He lived for his art. As far as he was concerned the only other members of the human race were the people who bought it. He might have stretched a point and included anyone who borrowed it, but no one borrowed books from the library any more. There were no books to borrow, only records and videos.

As soon as they came to power in the general election of '76, the Anti-Poets had ordered all libraries to sell their books to raise money to buy the records and videos. They were forbidden by Act of Parliament to buy other books with the proceeds. This, although he did not know it, was one of the reasons that Dagobert's slim volume, *Mollusc*, had failed. When he had peddled copies on street corners, destitute librarians had stood wringing their hands helplessly, crying, 'We dare not, do not tempt us. If we buy books for people to read, lightning will strike us.' He could not even bribe them with kippers.

One night, in The Frog's Legs, a group of librarians were huddled over their pints and furtively sharing an ode on a dogfish, freshly acquired from Dagobert.

'Poetry,' mourned one. 'Remember, we used to have whole shelves full.'

'Mmmm,' said Miss McCadaver, Chief Librarian with Special Responsibility for Nintendo, 'there is no embargo upon us buying fish, is there?' There was a murmur of astonished delight around the table.

'Are you suggesting,' said a colleague, 'that we restock with fish?'

'There is nothing in the statute book that prohibits a library from loaning fish,' said another.

This was the turning point. Slowly, not wishing to attract unwelcome attention, the librarians began to stack their denuded shelves with plaice, cod, sole, haddock, halibut. The Anti-Poets, who patrolled the libraries disguised as borrowers, noticed the fish, but not what was written upon them. The only problem was that the poems had a very short shelf-life, as Miss McCadaver pointed out to Dagobert when he arrived one morning to deliver a consignment of haiku tattooed on whitebait.

Dagobert was forced to agree. The atmosphere in the library reminded him of the early days when he was beneficiary of his cousin's will.

'Kippers,' he said.

'Is it possible to tattoo a kipper?' asked Miss McCadaver.

'No, but it was not so much kippering I was thinking of as the general principle of preservation. Can you install freezers?'

'We can do anything we like,' said Miss McCadaver, 'so long as we don't buy books.'

'And so literature was saved!' Elaine said. 'Deepfreeze cabinets replaced the book shelves.'

'Until the Anti-Poets privatised the libraries,' I said. 'That was the master stroke.'

'They floated the Library Service on the Stock Exchange.'

'Massive television campaign first. "Buy your library! *Own* your library." But the day the shares went on sale, no one turned up.'

'People didn't want to own their libraries?'

'Most of them thought that they owned them already. They seemed to recall seeing signs outside saying PUBLIC LIBRARY. We're the public aren't we? they thought, but when they went to check up they found that UBLIC had been painted out and RIVATE painted over the top, so they all went home again. The rest couldn't read anyway.'

'The Anti-Poets had infiltrated the Government. The front bench was packed with them. One after another they stood up and spoke, day after day. Force 15 on the Auger Scale.'

'Not a single share was purchased. The Anti-Poets said, "Oh, well, no one wants libraries after all," so they were all closed down.'

'What happened to Dagobert?' Elaine said.

'Tattooed himself to death and climbed into the freezer with the last of the fish, leaving an epitaph inscribed on a hake. But that was in the future,' I said. 'Don't forget, at this moment in time, Zoot Humus is still on the trail of the Illuminated Turbot.'

— 8 —
Soft Tissue Damage

Earth's fabric wore thinner. Now when I went about Compton Rosehay I could see the jostling outlines of Stalemate. The mermaid factory was in production, the Blackmail Co-operative flourished, increasing its numbers daily, the body bank in the car park was haunted by Lord Tod and Captain Cheeseheart, adding to their respective collections. The Martians initiated a massive revivalist crusade and made a thousand converts in a single evening, while the streets were thronged by the teeming Throats, the McCadaver clan and the Little Sisters of the Apocalypse, known familiarly as the Combat Nuns.

All through the Easter holiday Elaine and I revised for the coming exams, by day. In the evenings we walked in Stalemate.

A perpetual bone of contention between us was the exact nature of the apparitions at the London Road Roundabout, and we argued for a long time over who inhabited the tall detached house in Mockbeggar, known to us as Glanders. It was one of the genuinely old ones, a relic of the original Rosehay village, and unlike most of its fellow survivors it had not been enlarged with extensions and loft conversions. On the contrary, it appeared to have been made smaller, for on both of the side walls were the inverted Vs that marked where other, lower roofs had once been joined on.

'Clearly,' Elaine said, 'whoever lives there is notably anti-social. Once upon a time it was part of a row, but the owner detested the proximity of neighbours so much that he crept out one night and dynamited the houses on either side.'

It was an anti-social looking house. There was the height, for a start, three storeys above the ground and a basement area below street level. The removal of whatever buildings had once flanked it had left it, very unusually for Stalemate, with gardens at the side as well as at the back. There was easily room for another house to have been squeezed in on either side.

Now, squeezing in other houses was what the natives of Stalemate were good at. Even in streets where the houses were detached they were built so close together that there was scarcely room for a fence between them. They were narrow houses inhabited, we decided, by lean, sidling people who had lost the ability to put one foot in front of the other and were mainly employed to clean behind the tanks in the mermaid factory. What made Glanders remarkable was the fact that houses had actually been taken out.

'Obviously it was built by sociable people, in a terrace,' Elaine explained as we strolled along Osier Bank. 'For centuries it was one of a neighbourly row, but then, in '76—'

'—after the Nuns' riot—'

'—isolationists moved in.'

'The Plantagenets?'

'I don't think so,' Elaine said, pensively. 'After all, they aren't just exiles, they're keeping their heads down. Not even the neighbours know who they are. One day all will be revealed, but they aren't drawing attention to themselves right now. They wouldn't risk drawing attention to themselves by living in a place like Glanders. People would talk—by the way, there's been another sighting of Richard III.'

'Reading?'

'Uh huh. Services Area at Watford Gap.'

Glanders stood opposite the junction where Starve-acre ran into Mockbeggar. We turned right into Starveacre to get back to Coldharbour and walked alongside a high, featureless brick wall with pad-locked gates in it. There was no evidence to disprove Elaine's theory that this was where Lord Tod stored corpses surplus to his requirements and we always walked past it as quickly as we could, but that day I looked back. At the end of the road, somehow accentuated by the perspective of the brick wall, Glanders towered above the surrounding roofs, bland, flat-faced. No bay window broke the planes of its walls, no dormer protruded from the roof. In spite of its size it was, for Stalemate, a remarkably dull house. At that moment, I knew what had hap-pened.

'It was the neighbours,' I said.

'What neighbours?'

'Who pulled down the houses on either side—tore them down in a frenzy when the death count rose to double figures. He had to be stopped. They had to isolate him.'

'Who? What had he done?'

'Auger. Remember Auger, the most boring man in the world?'

'The man responsible for the Auger scale of tedium, up there with Richter and Beaufort.'

'That's him. No one noticed at first . . .'

No one noticed at first except the man who lived next door and even then it did not occur to him that Auger was responsible. After all, Auger was affable enough, always ready for a chat and, in the early days, before Auger really hit his stride, the effect was scarcely noticeable.

The man next door was called Smith, a name

which was, by Stalemate standards, quite strikingly ordinary. He himself had always regarded it as rather a dull name, boring even, and sometimes considered changing it to Smythe, or Smith-Smith, or Bladderbury, but when the facts emerged it was understood that Smith and his name might be dull, normal, average, uninteresting, unexciting, uninspiring, weary, flat, unprofitable and stale; but not boring. Auger was boring. Auger set the standards by which bores would be judged for ever more.

Smith was a clerical assistant at the mermaid factory, a quiet man of modest habits, whose only recreations were gardening and, occasionally, a game of darts at The Slug and Bottle where he would repair of an evening for a glass of mineral water. Had someone like the lawyer Jones or Zoot Humus or Professor Scrapie lived next door to Auger, the Glanders Effect might have been noticed sooner and lives saved. Scrapie would have written to the *Times*. What Jones and Humus would have done hardly bears thinking about, but Fate willed it otherwise. Smith was the hero of the hour.

One Sunday morning, soon after Auger moved in to Glanders, Mr Smith was walking along his straight garden path, examining his rosebuds for greenfly, when he noticed his new neighbour standing on the other side of the fence, regarding him fixedly.

'Pleasant morning,' Smith remarked.

'Funny you should say that,' Auger replied. 'Only just now I was thinking to myself which, when you come to analyse it, is almost invariably how one does think, since thinking is not an inter-active function but one which is normally carried out exclusively by the brain in the privacy of one's head, without oral communication—oral, that is, spelt o-r-a-l not aural spelt a-u-r-a-l which refers to the performance of those organs known as ears, though of course oral spelt o-r-a-l functions are entirely useless without reciprocal aural spelt a-u-r-a-l functions. Quite a coincidence, really.'

'Quite,' said Smith, thinking to himself, This man is clearly an intellectual. I do not understand a word he is saying.

'But then life as we know it is fraught with coincidences,' Auger was remarking. 'Take the fact that this pleasant, as you so accurately described it, morning, that is, that period of the diurnal span that precedes noon, both of us should happen to be standing in exactly the same spot upon our respective garden paths. Were it not for the truly amazing intervention of providence, I should have, at this precise moment, been standing seven and one half feet farther from my back door. Prior to quitting the house, through the said door, I was about to switch on my Rowenta automatic electric jug kettle for the purposes of infusing a cup of tea when I came in again, when it occurred to me that it would be more economical to decant the surplus water, since I required, being a bachelor and living, as it were, alone, only one cup of tea, and as I was about to unplug the device, since it is excessively perilous to handle live electrical equipment, especially in the vicinity of H_2O, that is, *water* . . .'

Smith, who had been staring at Auger all this time, half-mesmerized, had the distinct impression that his corneas were solidifying.

'I think I heard my phone ringing,' he said, making as if to retreat back up the garden to the house.

'. . . distracted by the sight of an uncommonly fascinating brick which was lying—in fact still *is* lying, bricks being, in the main, inert and incapable of voluntary locomotion— exactly half-way along the third course from the base of the hard standing upon which my greenhouse was at some time, although not by myself, erected. It was to view this noble brick that I betook myself from the kitchen sink, though had it not been for my deliberations upon the water level in the automatic jug kettle, I should have by now been seven and one half feet beyond the point where we are presently stationary, and communing with my brick. Allow me to delineate its salient features—'

Or possibly he's mad, thought Smith. He went upstairs and looked out of his back bedroom window which gave a clear view of both his own garden and the one next door. Auger was still standing on his patio, discoursing upon brickwork, apparently oblivious to the fact that Smith was not only no longer listening to him but no longer there. After a few minutes Auger, who was still talking, turned ponderously and went indoors. Smith, who could lip read, distinctly made out the words: 'It really is extraordinary how attractive one's voice sounds to other people.'

Soon afterwards Smith heard Auger's front door open and close, and deemed it safe to venture into the garden again. He looked cautiously over the fence, which seemed to have splintered unaccountably here and there, although he had erected it only a few weeks previously. Auger's garden was completely bare. The house had stood empty for several months before he moved in and the lawn of Glanders had become very overgrown. Now there was no sign of it, no grass at all, simply bare earth from which a couple of withered weeds protruded. Numerous earthworms lay dead upon the surface.

He must have used a potent weed killer, Smith thought, and began to be worried about the effect that this might have had upon his own garden. As far as he could see no plants had died although in the vegetable plot the runner beans seemed to be wilting, but that could be ascribed to the dry weather they had been enjoying.

Next afternoon, however, the runner beans were looking very sickly indeed and several young pods had fallen off.

'I've just been listening to Prime Minister's Question Time on the wireless,' said a voice, breathless with excitement, from the other side of the fence. 'I really can't understand how those fellows can sit through it day after day without rising to their feet and cheering. Don't you find politicians endlessly fascinating? When I see television pictures of the House of Commons in session my heart positively leaps; those rows of fresh, eager faces, those great minds, unsullied by any thought of personal profit, dedicated to the service of the nation—which, the nation that is, has become known as The Mother of Parliaments although many people are under the erroneous impression that Westminster itself is The Mother of Parliaments—'

Out of the corner of his eye Mr Smith became aware that his favourite hybrid tea rose, *Doctor Crippen*, had pulled itself up by the roots and was feebly and furtively trying to drag itself away. Two or three sweet peas, being planted farther from the fence and therefore less affected, were creeping towards the far side of the garden on the tips of their tendrils.

It was the following morning, when Smith made his customary inspection of the vegetable plot, that he noticed the fresh feathery tops of several of his young carrots were lying lethargically upon the soil. He seized hold of one of them and tugged. It came away in his hand. Where the healthy golden root of the carrot should have been there was a pool of gelid slime. An insistent droning sound, which he might otherwise have imagined to be the drowsy hum of summer bees, proclaimed the presence of Auger, on his back doorstep, remarking upon the texture of concrete paving slabs.

'If I had my way,' Auger was saying, 'all public libraries and museums would be obliged by statute to reserve a special area for the exhibition of paving slabs, with a resident curator to conduct school parties around the works on display. Mankind has for generations failed to appreciate the aesthetic properties of pre-cast concrete. Why, with my very fingertips, eyes closed, I can derive as much cerebral stimulations from exploring the surface of a paving slab as many men and, indeed, women, although I use the word "man" to refer to mankind, that is, humans in general, irrespective of sex, which word, I might add, does not, as many people suppose, refer to the *activity* but to the significant differences between those who engage in it, by which I mean, of course, male and female . . .'

As he watched, Smith saw another carrot keel over.

It's him, he thought. It's Auger. First the beans, then the rose and the sweet peas, now the carrots. Where has his grass gone? What killed the earth worms? Why is my new larch-lap fence beginning to disintegrate although I purchased it only six weeks ago and coated it thoroughly with creosote? What about that crack in my bathroom wall which was not there when I dusted last Thursday?

'... would get from watching the performance of a drama by the poet Shakespeare. Why pay vast sums of money, I ask myself, to watch actors, in which term I incorporate those members of the Thespian profession who take the feminine gender; gender that is, as opposed to sex ...'

Smith began to keep a diary. Day by day he logged the havoc that Auger was wreaking upon his garden. The lawn was turning brown, all the roses had wrenched themselves from the bed by the fence and were huddled against the potting shed on the far side of the patio. The runner beans had died and the root vegetables, following the example of the carrots, had absorbed their own tissues and degenerated into pools of gelid slime. Trees began to shed their bark the minute Auger appeared on his back doorstep and Smith discerned a deep crack appear in the brickwork where his house was joined to Glanders.

He called his observations The Glanders Effect and when a fine walnut at the end of the garden was discovered leafless and lifeless one morning, he resolved to alert the authorities to the problem, a resolution confirmed when, after twenty minutes of light conversation with Auger over the fence, Smith's eyelashes fell out, followed by his beard.

It was only when he took his findings to the Town Hall that Smith realized that he was not alone in his suspicions. The entire area was becoming susceptible to The Glanders Effect. Pressure was mounting. Two people were found inexplicably dead on the pavement outside Glanders, and in very bad condition. The Public Health Inspector was called in to compile statistics, to which end Smith's diary proved invaluable, and the council regularly debated ways of combating The Glanders Effect. Meanwhile the inhabitants of the neighbourhood were ready to take matters into their own hands when an off-duty police constable fell dead from his bicycle while passing Glanders.

'He was a popular man,' said the Chief Superintendent. 'This is a senseless crime.' He was right. By this time the entire street was senseless.

The data-gathering grew apace, Smith and the Public Health Inspector working round the clock to find the conclusive proof that they were looking for. As the house on the other side of Glanders had become mysteriously vacant, the occupants having either decamped or dissolved, the PHI moved in and, with Smith, commenced systematic monitoring. At last they could lay their theory before the authorities.

Waves of boredom were emanating from Glanders. The frequency would increase as the day wore on, peaking at around five o'clock in the afternoon. At first it was assumed that levels would fall to zero at night, probably by 2 a.m., but it was pointed out by Smith that if Auger had been dreaming, dead bats would be found littering the garden at dawn.

The lawyer Jones and Zoot Humus were consulted finally in the hope of finding some crime for which Auger could be arrested, charged, tried, sentenced and put out of circulation in a lead-lined cell, but again and again they failed. *There is no law which forbids boring people to death.*

'If there was,' Elaine said, 'just think how many

people would be off the streets: politicians, evangel-
ists, teachers—'
  'Chat-show hosts, yoof presenters—'
  'Comedians, sports personalities—'
  'Sports commentators—'
  'You could sue people for boring you. If they
refused to stop after a caution, they could be taken
to court and receive custodial sentences.'
  'Exactly,' I said, 'but that was just the problem.
Most boring is done in public. One is in the presence
of the bore, or at least in earshot. Auger could do it
in complete isolation, like radio-active waste.'
  'So how did they nail him the end?'

In the end the public took the law into their own
hands. When the death count reached double figures,
tempers frayed. Also, cracks were appearing in the
foundations of adjacent houses. Then, on New Year's
Eve, Auger had a nightmare and downed a light
aircraft that happened to be flying over Glanders. The
pilot's injuries could not be attributed solely to his
plunging from 15000 feet. To be precise, they were
exactly what you would expect to find in someone
who had plunged from 15000 feet, only the pilot had
come down by parachute. Why, therefore, was he
simply a bag of skin awash with a kind of primaeval
soup? It was The Glanders Effect, force 15 on the
Auger scale. That was when the neighbours rushed
out and demolished the houses on either side of Glanders. Smith was rendered temporarily homeless but
was rehoused by public subscription, in recognition
of his work and the thousands of lives which were
saved thereby. When the Auger scale was published
he received international recognition and was finally
awarded the Nobel Prize for Perseverance. It had
taken him a long while to calibrate precisely, but
these days it is hard to imagine how we could manage

without it. For a start, the Palace of Westminster is fitted with tedium detectors which flash red warnings when force 5 is reached. Otherwise the majority of MPs would die on the floor of the House and Big Ben would long ago have fallen into the Thames.

The Auger Scale
Force 1. Herbaceous plants wither.
Force 2. Autophagy in root vegetables.
Force 3. Trees shed bark.
Force 4. Metal fatigue.
Force 5. Structural damage to buildings.
Force 6. Facial hair falls out.
Force 7. Warts, corns and scabs detach
     spontaneously. Boils burst.
Force 8. Lesions in the epidermis. Gas mains
     rupture.
Force 9. Soft tissue damage.
Force 10. Sinovial fluid solidifies around joints.
     Diesel engines seize up.
Force 11. Human brain becomes smooth. Eyes melt.
Force 12. Bones disintegrate. Molecular structure of
     Uranium alters irreversibly.
Force 13. Major blood vessels rupture.
Force 14. Vital organs implode.
Force 15. Human brain liquefies.

'What happened to Auger in the end?' Elaine said.
  'What do you think?'
  'Well, was he visibly affected by what he had done?'
  'Not *visibly*. After a couple of months confined to his own company the inevitable happened,' I said. 'He bored himself to death. They never found the corpse.'
  'Lord Tod?'

'A viscid stain at the foot of the stairs.'
'Primaeval soup?'
'Naturally.'

— 9 —
Predictable Results
of a
Peace Conference

Towards the end of the holiday, when we ought to have been concentrating all our thoughts on going back to school and getting psyched up for the coming exams, Elaine and I sat in Jangles, locked once more in dispute about the apparitions at the London Road Roundabout. We both knew that neither of us was sufficiently interested in the apparitions ever to find out exactly what they were, they were just something that was referred to from time to time, like the Combat Sisters or Captain Cheeseheart. Captain Cheeseheart was not really Mr Lomax, Head of Lower School, he just shared the same space that was occupied by Mr Lomax which at least gave him a kind of substance lacked by the apparitions.

'Dagobert saw a cloud of blinding white light,' I reminded Elaine, 'from which a voice spoke unto him. According to Ernest Giblets it was a shower of small edible larvae accompanied by a halo round the moon.'

'Whereas Nigel McCadaver received explicit details about how and where he should stage his experimental theatre venture.'

'Which he would have done better to ignore,' I added. Nigel's theatrical experience, entitled *The Echoing Gut*, had been produced with a cast of one hundred and fifty on the steps of Stalemate Town Hall, featuring special effects by The Great Trochanter (from the bicycle shop), an Anatolian Ear Music Ensemble, a heavy metal mime show, monologues by Nigel accompanying himself on a foot-operated bagpipe and a troupe of nude bungee-jumpers who launched themselves from the topmost pinnacle of the Halifax Building Society. The event had been a resounding failure since the citizens of Stalemate, going about their business, had noticed nothing unusual and fiercely resented being asked to pay £10 for a ticket to watch what they regarded as every-day life in provincial England. Experimental theatre, to Stalemate, meant *The Sound of Music* on a pro-scenium stage.

'Nigel could have staged *The Sound of Music*,' I said, 'with real nuns. The Little Sisters of the Apoca-lypse would have been pleased to join in.'

'Prior to the Great Riot of '76. After that they had other things on their minds.'

We were in neutral gear, engines idling, for at the next table, taking great pains to look at us pityingly from time to time, were the Gang of Three. We had discovered from past experience that it was danger-ous to become too involved with Stalemate when there was anyone around to overhear us. Usually we found that Stalemate worked best when we were walking, but if the weather was too rough we went to Elaine's house where no one took any notice of us and we could spend all day investigating the trials of Dagobert and the Anti-Poets, or compiling the Auger scale. Paul had actually been in the same room when Nigel McCadaver saw the angel with the fiery sword materialize at the roundabout. I never took Elaine to my house although I pointed it out one day as we walked down Coldharbour. Elaine took one look at our satellite dish and observed that Aliens in the home were becoming a serious problem these days. Had I read that article in *Woman's Own* on how to deal with them? You could buy humane traps by mail order from the *Innovations* catalogue.

Watching Rowena, Marie and Lynzi watching *us*, I knew that we were acquiring a reputation. You do not have to do much in order to appear eccentric in Compton Rosehay and we had done plenty. This was all right for Elaine, who would move on and leave the reputation behind her like the discarded skin sloughed by a python. I would have to stay and live with my reputation, and with Elaine. I knew that the Gang of Three talked about us, not only to each other but to anyone else who would listen. When school began again in a couple of days, we would be going back as the class nutters. The real trouble was not just that Stalemate was meaningless to anyone who overheard it, but that if we, or at least I, knew that we had been overheard, it seemed to ring untrue. If only Elaine had not let slip, in Lynzi's hearing, that remark about angels causing vapour trails and who would have thought that heaven would look quite so much like Stansted Airport?

Rowena's crowd seemed set for the afternoon. In the end it was Elaine and I who fought our way out into the gale and hail of an April afternoon and went to sit in the arcade of The Cloister on the very spot, as it happened, where also stood the Convent of the Little Sisters of the Apocalypse.

'Affectionately known as the Combat Sisters since the Great Riot of '76,' Elaine reminded me. 'There may only be one convent in Stalemate now, but once there were three.'

'All within artillery range of each other,' I said.

'Exactly,' Elaine said. 'You can imagine what it was like.' I began imagining. 'It was bad enough on ordinary days; you could scarcely move without tripping over a nun doing good works. During festivals it was mayhem, religious processions clashing in the town centre, sacred relics hijacked, not to mention the Martians holding counter-demonstrations and demanding equal air-time for *their* holy relic. People began complaining.'

'Professor Scrapie wrote to the *Times*.'

'The Bishop summoned the three Mothers Superior to a summit conference in the hope that they would agree to divide Stalemate between them. It was a failure.'

'In the grounds of the Convent of the Apocalypse,' I said, intending to maintain duel control on this particular story, 'is an equestrian statue.'

'Our Lady on Horseback?'

'Reverend Mother Maria de los Angeles, mailed *cap-à-pie* and riding her destrier, Nightgown, down the main street of Stalemate to quell the Great Riot of '76.'

'Well, anyway,' Elaine said. 'Let's get back to the beginning. The summit conference . . .'

It was the Bishop of Stalemate who called the summit conference after a particularly nasty incident in which barricades were erected and missals thrown. The principal delegates were Reverend Mother Methuselah from the Convent of the Poor Things and Reverend Mother Doreen from Stalemate Urban District Convent. Reverend Mother Maria de los Angeles from the Convent of the Apocalypse prudently declined to attend and sent her envoy, Sister Eclampsia, but in addition to these three they brought with them their retinues of bodyguards, intelligence officers, translators, personal assistants and press officials. When they finally sat down to negotiate they were seventy-six at table, not counting the Bishop. They spent two days arguing about who should speak first, and since neither of the Mothers Superior would speak to each other or to Sister Eclampsia, everything had to be written down, passed to a translator and read out in a more tactful form. Finally the Bishop was able to put his peace plan before them. Taking advantage of the fact that

Stalemate was perfectly circular, he had divided the map into three, like a pie chart, each sector to be under the exclusive jurisdiction of its particular convent, and with a small demilitarized zone in the middle which enclosed Lord Tod's demesne, the four pubs and the Martian Temple.

'Perfectly equitable,' said the Bishop, but he had reckoned without Reverend Mother Doreen.

'What about amenities?' she shrieked. 'All the shops are in the Poor Things' zone. We demand access to the shops.'

At this, Reverend Mother Methuselah rose up pointing a trembling finger.

'So!' she screamed. 'We have the shops! What use are shops to us? We do not purchase, we beg alms. There are no *houses* in our zone. Who do we beg from?'

Up got Sister Eclampsia. 'Beg from people who are out shopping,' she said. 'In our zone we have neither shops nor houses. Are we complaining?'

'What have you got to complain about?' demanded Reverend Mother Doreen. 'It's common knowledge that you have massive investment in the oil trade and multinational pharmaceuticals!'

'Moreover,' said Reverend Mother Methuselah, 'your zone controls all the exits and entrances to Stalemate. You have the bus station. You have the London Road Roundabout and the railway. Even if we control the shops there is no assurance that the Little Sisters of the Apocalypse will allow food into other zones.'

'Trade routes can be guaranteed,' the Bishop began soothingly, but at that point Sister Norah, intelligence officer from the Urban District Convent, leapt from her seat with a wild scream.

'It's a plot! It's a plot! They are planning to bring in an interdenominational peacekeeping force. We shall be swamped by Unitarians, Anabaptists, Plymouth Brethren, Latter-day Saints, Wee Frees, Peculiar People -!'

'Treachery! Treachery!' A sister of the Poor Things, frothing at the mouth, snatched the Bishop's map from the wall and ripped it into three sections, scornfully rending the carefully calculated zones.

'We spit on your peace plan,' she cried. 'Before we know where we are the Americans will send in military advisers and we all know where *that* will lead.'

The cry went up from every throat. 'Back to your convents, sisters, and prepare for war.'

Unknown to the Bishop, all three convents had already made contingency plans. When the peace conference broke down, as they fully intended it should, disguised novices on fast bicycles had sped back to report on events, without waiting for further instructions. When the doors of the Bishop's palace burst open and the seventy-six delegates stormed out, the three convents flung wide their gates simultaneously and the sisters poured forth into the town armed with billhooks and holy water.

Reverend Mother Maria de los Angeles went to the topmost tower of her convent and after praying briefly for peace looked in dismay at the terrifying sight of three hundred rioting nuns in the street. There was no time to be lost. She spun on her spurred heel and raced clanking downstairs. Under her habit she wore a suit of plate armour, cuirass, grieves and gauntlets. Over her wimple she jammed her plumed helmet, slammed down the visor and strode to the stables where Sister Orthodontia, whose wooden leg prevented her from marching with her sisters, was leading out the redoubtable Nightgown, saddled and caparisoned, harness clinking with holy medals. Reverend Mother Maria de los Angeles sprang to the saddle. Sister Orthodontia placed in her hand the sword of St Hugh the Bleeder of Bruges. She raised it high and rode with stately clangour towards the gate and out in Sennacre. Nightgown's ebony quarters gathered to spring into a gallop, fifteen hundredweight of horseflesh and twenty stones of Reverend Mother Maria de los Angeles in full armour.

But what is this? Reverend Mother checks the reins. Nightgown goes down on her haunches and paws the air with forefeet like pile drivers—

'Isn't Nightgown a magnificent black stallion?' Elaine objected.

'In a convent? Get real,' I said. 'Anyway, there on the corner of Goat's Lea she halted. Nightgown brought down her hooves and lowered her head submissively. Reverend Mother looked questioningly across the street at Number 15, the one with lace curtains and geraniums on the window-sill. The curtains moved in a mysterious way.'

'Who lives at Number 15?' Elaine asked.

'Who do you think?' I said. 'God.'

'In there? All of him?'

'The works. After he had finished creating Stalemate he was just walking away, whistling quietly – '

'To Stansted Airport – '

' —when he was surrounded by indignant citizens. "Oh no you don't," they said. "You built it, you live in it." He's been here ever since.'

Anyway, Reverend Mother stopped there, in the middle of the road, the sunshine gilding her helmet and drawing white light from the gleaming blade of the sword of St Hugh the Bleeder. After a bit the Archangel Gabriel came out.

'Is right on my side?' said Reverend Mother Maria de los Angeles, and Gabriel went back in.

'Now what does she want?' said God, who was peering under the curtains, between the geraniums.

'Wants to know if right's on her side,' said Gabriel.

'Well, I suppose it had better be,' said God. 'After all, I'm on the side of the big battalions and they don't come any bigger than Reverend Mother.'

'You could try backing the losers for once,' Gabriel said.

'Why stir things up?' said God. 'Anyway, if I backed the losers they wouldn't *be* losers, would they?' So Gabriel nipped out again and said, 'Go for it, Sister!' and Reverend Mother whirled the Bleeder's sword three times round her head, cried 'Hi-yo, Nightgown!' and charged down Sennacre, Nightgown's hooves striking fiery sparks from the cobblestones.

'Better go and see what she's up to,' God said, so Gabriel left him at the window and went out the back way, got his bike from the shed and followed Nightgown, pedalling madly. It was an old Raleigh with a basket on the handlebars. He'd given up ten-speeds because they kept getting nicked. Normally he could get fifteen miles an hour out of it but now he was riding into a head wind, Reverend Mother's slipstream; his wings spread; he had lift-off. Over the heaving throng he sailed, still pedalling. The throng stopped heaving—everyone looked up as his huge Boeing-shaped shadow came between them and the sun. He soared and spiralled, having found a thermal, round and round, up and up. The inevitable happened. At 15000 feet he let go of the handlebars—the bike was upsetting his trim and causing him to yaw—without thinking of the consequences. Gabriel was still going up, but the bike was coming down. It twisted in the air, like a falling cat preparing to land on its feet. Miraculously the bell began to ring. The pedals were still turning. The spinning wheels activated the dynamo and from the front lamp an unearthly light flooded the upturned faces below. Hypnotized they stood gazing as the bicycle descended inexorably. They were still there when it landed.

The death count was two hundred and thirty-seven. Three were directly under the bicycle, the rest were due to the domino effect. The intersection of Sennacre and Copsewood was entirely blocked by flattened nuns. The shock wave broke windows as far away as the mermaid factory, in fact several tanks were damaged and one mermaid had to be terminated.

The proprietor of the mermaid factory, Obadiah Gleet, made a tremendous fuss and threatened to sue. Reverend Mother Maria de los Angeles remarked that if he intended to sue the Archangel Gabriel he was going to have his work cut out, but agreed to admit four of his surplus mermaids to her order as postulants, partly in order to pacify him, partly because she wanted to replenish her depleted numbers, since fifteen Sisters of the Apocalypse had succumbed to the bicycle.

This was not the least of her worries. The two remaining convents had been completely wiped out and suddenly the sisters found time hanging heavy on their hands. They had Stalemate to themselves, without opposition. There need be no more secret forays by night, no raiding parties, no ambushing of rival sisters. For a fortnight an uneasy calm hung over the convent and then, one morning, shortly after Nones, Sister Orthodontia came stumping up the back stairs on her wooden leg to report that sandbags had appeared in the corridor leading to the refectory. Reverend Mother Maria de los Angeles did not normally wear armour indoors but she paused to slip a lightweight cuirass under her scapular before hurrying down to investigate. By the time she arrived, the barricade of sandbags had risen to shoulder height opposite the foot of the main staircase. Across the top of it peered Sisters Marilyn and Billie-Jean, flak-helmets over their wimples.

'*Pax vobiscum*,' Reverend Mother said, automatically.

'Why do you go about saying Peace, Peace, when there is no peace?' Sister Billie-Jean demanded, and Reverend Mother heard the unmistakable click of a safety-catch released.

'Why should there not be peace?' asked Reverend Mother, and her fingers itched for the friendly feel of the pommel of the sword of St Hugh the Bleeder of Bruges.

'We want those mermaids out of here,' Sister Marilyn said. 'They are enjoying privileges denied to the rest of us.'

'That is outright tailism,' Reverend Mother protested. 'The only advantages, if they can be described as such, enjoyed by our new sisters, are the castors.'

At that moment, from behind her, the sound of murmurous whirring filled the corridor, punctuated by rhythmic slaps, and the four young mermaids glided into view. Because of their understandable problems in moving about the convent, Sister Sciatica, in the metalwork shop, had constructed lightweight aluminium crinolines which the mermaids wore under their habits. Attached to the bases of the crinolines were sets of castors, the entire contraption propelled by the muscular tail as it struck the floor, thus accounting for the slapping sounds. The snout of Billie-Jean's Uzi appeared above the sandbags.

'They started it,' Sister Marilyn said. 'They are demanding unrestricted access to the whole of the ground floor.'

'But sisters, you already have unrestricted access

to the whole of the ground floor,' Reverend Mother appealed to the mermaids, only then noticing that two of them were carrying between them a substantial bale of barbed wire.

'We are restricted by the presence of the other sisters,' declared Sister Barnacle. '*They* have access to the entire building. *We* are confined to this one floor. We demand that all plantigrade sisters withdraw to the first and second storeys.'

While Sister Barnacle was opening negotiations, Sisters Sargasso and Doldrum were erecting barbed wire entanglements across the foot of the main staircase.

'The back stairs are already a no-go area,' said the fourth mermaid, Sister Flotsam. 'We have secured the fire escape. Safe conduct is offered to all sisters on their way upstairs. You have until midnight. If anyone with feet remains down here after the ultimatum expires, we cannot be answerable for the consequences.'

'And how do you suppose that we shall get in and out,' demanded Billie-Jean, 'once the stairs are cut off?'

'That is your problem,' said Sister Barnacle. 'Ladders, firemen's poles, parachutes . . . You have brought this upon yourselves. Ever since we first arrived we have had to endure whispered insults about fish-brains, fins, gills and swim bladders. Since we got the castors, I might add,' she cried, rounding on Reverend Mother Maria de los Angeles, 'we have been renamed Sister Tram, Sister Trolley, Sister Dalek and Sister Hovercraft. We didn't come here to be insulted.'

'Tell me, what's to stop us blowing you away, Sister?' inquired Sister Marilyn who was, Reverend Mother now observed, staggering under the burden of a grenade launcher.

'Blow away all you like,' retorted Sister Flotsam. 'Blow us to kingdom come if that's where your heart lies; just remember that wheresoever we are blown, you will be coming with us.'

Something, at this point, caused Reverend Mother to look downwards, whereupon she noticed wires trailing from under Sister Sargasso's habit. There was a possibility, she mused, that the young mermaid was plugged into the mains, somewhere, thus facilitating her movements about the convent, but silently her lips formed the words, 'Booby-trap?'

'I'm the trap, guess who's the booby,' Sister Sargasso replied, laconically. 'First time anyone looses off, the whole place goes up.'

Round the bend in the stairs came a procession of nuns led by Sister Eclampsia who was carrying a banner. 'We declare solidarity with our fishy sisters,' she announced, in ringing tones. 'We claim the moral ground floor.' The renegades filed silently through the aperture in the barbed wire and formed a semi-circle round the four mermaids. 'Even now,' continued Sister Eclampsia, 'Sister Sciatica, under armed guard, is converting vehicles for our use. Down with feet!'

As she spoke, a jangling clatter broke out in the distance and along the corridor came Sister Sciatica, pushing a train of baggage trolleys, each bearing the legend *Not to be removed from Stansted Airport*. As one nun, the renegades swooped upon the train crying, 'Down with feet!' and each detached a trolley and leapt aboard. The trolleys, under Sciatica's expert hand, had been equipped with a kind of punt pole and instantly the corridor was surging with milling sisters, except for Sargasso who, white-lipped and defiant, stood at the foot of the stairs, one rigid arm pointing wordlessly at the wires that snaked from beneath her crinoline.

By midnight it was all over. Sister Sargasso, who had stood her ground for thirteen hours, severed her wires with bolt cutters and with the other three mermaids set about demolishing Sister Billie-Jean's machine-gun post. All night the victorious Piscean Faction, as they now called themselves, caroused in a most sacred manner and then, when the sun rose, sallied forth on their wheels to inflict good works upon the natives of Stalemate, leaving only Sister Eclampsia to guard the staircase.

The moment the last trolley was out of sight, Sister Eclampsia put two fingers in her mouth, emitting a shrill whistle, which was instantly answered by Sister Sciatica who had been in her confidence all along.

'You mean Eclampsia was a double agent!' Elaine gasped.

'No less,' I said, savouring the triumph of having sprung a surprise although, as was the way in Stalemate, I had not known that Sister Eclampsia was playing a double game until I said it.

At first she fully intended to throw in her lot with the Piscean Faction, but overnight her ardour cooled as she watched the mermaids flood the refectory and issue orders that henceforth all activities would be carried out under water, and that nothing was to be eaten except kelp and a kind of primaeval soup which Sister Sargasso insisted was rich in plankton. After that, Sister Eclampsia had no trouble deciding where her loyalties lay.

While the Pisceans were out and about Stalemate, the remnant of the Combat Sisters regained possession of the ground floor, but the seeds of mistrust had been sown. Although for a time they stood shoulder to shoulder to repel the Pisceans, they were dividing into factions themselves. One group drained the refectory and claimed it for their own, while another faction took possession of the whole first floor and a splinter group holed up on the second. Reverend Mother Maria de los Angeles and Sister Orthodontia, with a few faithful followers, proclaimed themselves the only true Sisters of the Apocalypse and appropriated the attics. Meanwhile dissent had broken out on the ground floor. Sisters Marilyn and Billie-Jean re-erected their machine-gun post and refused admission to any sister except on payment of a heavy toll. Within a year the convent had disintegrated entirely and each sister had mined her own cell and declared a personal republic.

This state of affairs persisted for some time until Reverend Mother Maria de los Angeles lost patience, got up early one morning and carried out a preemptive strike with the sword of Sir Hugh the Bleeder of Bruges. She then renamed the convent The Hermitage and had the place to herself.

'What about the Pisceans?'

'The mermaids found work as mermaids. The rest returned the baggage trolleys to Stansted and were never seen again—not as nuns, anyway.'

'And Nightgown, and Sister Orthodontia?'

'They escaped the sword of Sir Hugh and set up an order of their own – '

'Called the Quinquepedalians,' Elaine chipped in. 'It consisted of five feet. Correct me if I'm wrong, but wasn't it *Saint* Hugh the Bleeder?'

'He was a humble knight to begin with,' I explained. 'Plain Sir Hugh; but after going on a crusade he was canonized for services to Christianity. Slaughtered thousands—in a most holy manner, of course.'

—10—
A Bad Case
of Democracy

Although it was now officially the Summer Term the wind had backed round to the east again, off the North Sea, and the chain link fence inside the conifer hedge was plastered with debris that had been swept from the school field. Sweet wrappers and crisp packets crackled fretfully as we walked alongside; the conifers heaved and whispered.

'Of course, it's not a hedge at all,' Elaine remarked, 'it's a quango; a quasi-governmental body set up after the last election to report on subversive elements trying to enter Stalemate from outside.'

'The Anti-Poets again?' I said. 'Surely they wouldn't put their trust in trees?'

'Trees which are regularly cut down to size,' Elaine reminded me. 'These buggers would grow up to 30 metres, left to get on with it.'

The chief characteristic of the Anti-Poets, we had discovered, was their hatred of trees. In fact, it was only Dagobert the fishmonger poet who referred to them as Anti-Poets because, reasonably enough, it was the only thing he had noticed about them; gardeners and botanists had another name for them: Blighters.

'This then,' I said, 'accounts for the Glanders Effect forces 1—3 on the Auger scale: herbaceous plants wither, disintegration of root vegetables, trees shed bark. Auger was the first of the Anti-Poets.'

'Or Blighters,' Elaine said. 'I'm not so sure about that. Auger was disinterested; there is no proof that he acted with malice aforethought. The truth of the matter is that once the Blighters became aware of the

Glanders Effect they saw it as a means to their own fell ends. The Stalemate Gardening Club and Botanical Society couldn't fail to notice that when certain persons were in the vicinity whole flower beds were laid waste, branches fell from mature trees, vegetable plots were converted into primaeval soup.'

'They drew up a list; people who were on no account to be invited into their gardens.'

'But it was trees that the Blighters hated especially; their age, their massive dignity, their towering indifference to political propaganda. The Blighters had had an unfortunate experience with trees. Back in '76 they had made a concerted effort and driven an Act through Parliament, enfranchising trees. Any tree over the age of eighteen was given the vote. At the next general election politicians thronged the streets announcing tree-oriented legislation – '

'Kissing saplings – '

' —they thought, you see, that trees were stupid. Since they could not read they would not know when they were being lied to.'

'As we know,' I said, 'from the trials of Dagobert the fishmonger poet, there were plans afoot to render the whole population of Stalemate illiterate.'

'But the trees were not stupid. They had been around a long time; most of the big ones had been around a lot longer than the Blighters. On polling day not a single tree turned up to vote. They simply stood about, where they always stood, staring down at the Blighters; and the Blighters, now thoroughly paranoiac, detected in the whispering of the leaves a note of supercilious scorn.'

'Which they resented. Only *they* were allowed to be supercilious and scornful.'

'In their view, everyone who disagreed with them had to be an idiot,' Elaine said. 'So it became second nature to sneer at the electorate and laugh pityingly when journalists asked them perfectly sensible questions.'

'They didn't admit that trees were worthy opponents?'

'Nobody was a worthy opponent. What did trees contribute to the gross national product? About as much as poets and actors and painters. Only valuable once they were dead.'

'Actors?'

'Nigel McCadaver's experimental theatre venture.'

'I hadn't realized the Blighters were behind that.'

'Behind everything,' Elaine said. 'Behind every failure, every disaster. What was happening to the trees was due – '

'What *was* happening to the trees?'

'Mass defoliation, ring-barking, fungal infections, Dutch Elm Disease . . . All this would have been blamed on natural phenomena had it not been for Ernest Giblets who had a very meaningful though Platonic relationship with a young copper beech. When it began to sicken, he called in a plant psychologist.'

Ernest Giblets was one of mine. A retired espionage operative, he was one of the few inhabitants of Stalemate who had, like Lord Tod, come from outside, originally settling here in order to recuperate from a life spent trying to destabilize other people's governments, to which end he had spent several years working for the CIA. I had not been aware that Ernest was interested in trees.

'Only in this particular tree,' Elaine explained. 'He raised it from seed . . .'

It was a beech nut which Ernest had brought back from a tour of duty in Central Europe. At first, when his tree failed to thrive, he assumed that it was suffering from cultural displacement; a Bulgarian tree growing up in an alien environment, but as he had no means of communicating with it, although he spoke Bulgarian, he finally sought the services of a psychologist. Naturally he could talk to the tree, as many others had done, but it could not answer him, at least, not in any way that he could understand, and it broke his heart to see it languishing pallidly in his front garden.

There were several psychologists listed in Yellow Pages, but only one practice that offered Anxiety and Depression Therapy for plants; Nostradamus, Nosferatu and Nostril. He made an appointment over the phone to see Nosferatu whose name appealed to him, as he saw at once that it was an anagram of Fear Not Us or, alternatively, Fur On Seat, and next morning went along to the address given, the converted bicycle shop next to the mermaid factory.

On entering the waiting room he found three other patients ahead of him; a potted parlour palm which was having a mid-leaf crisis, a hyper-sensitive plant and a basket of onions. He waited for an hour, meanwhile striking up a conversation with the man accompanying the onions.

'What's with the basket case?' Giblets asked.

'Infantilism. They won't grow.'

Another twenty minutes passed. Giblets became impatient. A begonia had come out of the consulting room with its minder, and the parlour palm had entered, but it was already long past the time for Giblets's appointment. He strode to the door. The receptionist, a tough cookie, leapt up to intercept him.

'I've been waiting eighty minutes,' Giblets cried, punctiliously. 'What kind of an appointment system do you call this?'

'The begonia is a very difficult subject and Dr Nostril has been called to an emergency case of bud blast. Dr Nostradamus is having to deal with *his* patients as well as his own. Only Dr Nosferatu is here with him and, in any case,' the receptionist said, 'why have you not brought the patient along with you?'

'Because it's nineteen feet high,' Giblets snapped, pushing past her.

'Then you should have asked for a house call!' It was too late. Giblets barged out of the waiting room, entangling fragrantly with a scented pelargonium which was on its way in, and flung open the nearest door. It was the wrong one. He burst in not on Dr Nosferatu but on Nostradamus. The psychologist was sitting with his back to the window. Lying on the couch was a Swiss Cheese plant, convulsively clutching its moss pole.

'Just relax your aerial roots,' the psychologist was saying, but the Swiss Cheese plant only gripped more tightly. Giblets could hear it whimpering from where he stood. Tiny beads of dew misted its leaves.

He backed out of the doorway, sweating. Was this the fate that awaited his copper beech? A steely arm was flung across his throat. It was the receptionist.

'Come back, you fool!' she cried. 'You could undo the painstaking work of months, crashing in like that. The Swiss Cheese plant is in analysis.'

Abashed, Giblets followed her back into the waiting room.

'What did you mean,' she asked, 'when you said that your patient is nineteen feet high? Is it a tree?'

'Copper beech,' Giblets said.

'Why didn't you say so?' she exclaimed. 'Dr Nostril is our tree man. Nostradamus and Nosferatu are the herbaceous specialists although Nostradamus will occasionally agree to help bulbs—if the bulbs really want to be helped.'

'The onions,' Giblets said.

'The onions, yes. I will tell Dr Nostril to call on you at the earliest opportunity.'

Ernest Giblets did not at all care for the looks of Dr Nostril when he saw him walking up the path next morning. The psychologist was short and greenish but, Giblets supposed, this latter attribute would no doubt engender a sense of security in his patients. Indeed, he had the distinct impression that as Nostril brushed against the leaves of a trailing ivy by the gate, the stems reached out tenderly to caress his boot. He advanced to meet the doctor, shook his verdant hand and conducted him to the side of the garden where the copper beech was drooping against the wall.

'Your patient,' Giblets said.

Nostril laid a hand upon the trunk of the copper beech. 'Name?' he said.

'It doesn't have a name,' Giblets said, 'it's a tree.'

'No name?' Nostril seemed aghast. 'Good Lord, man, how can you expect it to have any sense of identity, of intrinsic worth, of selfhood, if you don't even know its name?'

'I've always just called it "you",' Giblets confessed. 'It seemed to respond.'

'It isn't responding now,' Nostril said grimly. 'This could be a case of childhood deprivation. When were you first aware of the problem?'

'About three years ago, when it turned fifteen.'

'Adolescence is always fraught with problems,' said Nostril, 'traumatic enough in humans, but how much more so in a tree. Does it have many friends?'

'It seems to get on all right with those rhododendrons,' Giblets said. 'They're a raucous bunch, but good-hearted. No malice in them.'

'But it has no special friend, no confidant? With whom does it share its innermost thoughts, its dreams and hopes?'

'With me, I suppose,' Giblets said.

'I understood that there was no possibility of verbal communication between you.'

'I talk to it, and assume it understands. Conversely, I assume that it assumes that I can understand it when it talks to me,' said Giblets.

'It seems to me that you have been taking too much for granted,' Nostril said. 'Fetch me a step-ladder.'

Giblets did as he was ordered and retired to his living room from where he had a clear view of Nostril communing with his tree. The psychologist stood upon the topmost step of the ladder, his fingertips lightly touching the beech on either side of its trunk, just above where the first branches emerged, and with his head inclined so that one ear rested against the bark. He remained thus for a good hour and a half, while Giblets drank many nervous cups of black coffee and watched a county councillor on the far side of the road leaning over a garden wall to give a hollyhock a hard time. At last he observed that Nostril was descending and hurried into the garden.

'Tell me – ' he began, but Nostril took him by the shoulder and hustled him indoors.

'Not out there, where she can hear us,' he said.

'She?'

'Your tree. Her name is Hilary. Oh – ' a tear fell upon his beard which, Giblets now noticed, bore a remarkable resemblance to a mat of pine needles, ' – what a tale of despair and desolation I have heard. That tree has a serious inferiority complex. For one thing, on the other side of your fence is a silver birch which is ascending at the rate of two feet a year. I suggest that Hilary be moved immediately, which will be enormously expensive. Either that, or we will embark upon a course of therapy.'

'Which will also be enormously expensive?'

'Exorbitant,' Nostril agreed, cheerfully, 'but if you care for Hilary, and I believe that you do, in spite of your years of neglect, expense will be no object. She can be saved, man. You have only to give the word.'

'There is a third alternative,' Giblets said. 'You could teach me to understand her. In the long term that must surely be desirable. Or you could teach her to understand me.'

'You lay people always think you can do better than the professionals,' Nostril snapped. 'Do you really imagine that I could teach you in a matter of weeks what it has taken me years of meticulous study to learn—and I warn you, weeks is all we have. Delay any longer and it's bye-bye Hilary. Kindling. Chairlegs.'

'Let me think about it,' Giblets said. 'I have to consider ways of raising the money.'

'Would you hesitate if it were your wife's well-being at stake?'

'No, but let's be frank, Doctor, this isn't my wife. It's a tree. I'm very fond of it—her—Hilary, I raised her from seed. I hoped to see her grow to stately maturity before I popped off but, let us face it; you are demanding huge sums of money without any guarantee of success.'

'I can show you testimonials from grateful patients; a sequoia, a Norfolk Island pine, at least three *malus tschonoskii* now fruiting again after years of barrenness – '

'No,' said Giblets, 'you can show me grateful letters from their credulous owners. I can just about believe that a tree may be taught to talk, but I draw the line at learning to write. Call me a sceptic if you like, but that's exactly what I am. You've just spent ninety-five minutes at the rate of £100 an hour, standing on a step-ladder with your head in a tree. What proof do I have that anything of a clinical nature has taken place? You'll be suggesting hypnosis next.'

'Hypnosis only works with bulbs; not my field,' Nostril said, contemptuously. 'I leave you to think it over. You know where to find me but I warn you, again I warn you, time is not on our side. Wait too long and the damage will be irreversible.' He headed for the door, muttering. 'Some people are not fit to keep trees. I'll find my own way out.'

'You couldn't find your way out of a paper bag,' Giblets hissed at Nostril's departing back, and watched through the window as Nostril strode to his car, ignoring the importunate fronds of the trailing ivy. There was a sticker in the rear window that read, *A tree is for life, not just for Christmas.*

When the car had driven away Giblets went out into the garden with a heavy heart. The ladder was still in position and he mounted it until he stood where Nostril had stood, on the highest step. The branches creaked mournfully. The withered leaves touched his cheek.

'Speak to me, Hilary,' Giblets whispered. 'Tell me what you told Nostril. I swear I will try to understand. The man's a quack, a charlatan, he sees you only as a case history. For god's sake, Hilary, I *planted* you. I'm the nearest thing you have to a father. Speak.'

He nearly fell off the step-ladder when a voice, very close to his ear replied, 'I told you I'd be back. Have you reached a decision?'

Giblets froze. For a moment he thought the speaker must be Nostril who had stopped his car at the end of the road and returned on foot. Nostril, after all, was the only person to whom he owned a decision, but as he squinted cautiously round the curve of Hilary's slender trunk the figure he descried lurking

147

in the next garden was not that of the psychologist, nor was it addressing Hilary.

Beside the silver birch stood a tall, stout, male person in a long dark overcoat, upon the lapel of which crouched, like a malevolent cabbage, a rosette. Giblets stifled a gasp. It was a politician.

'Resistance will get you nowhere,' the voice continued. 'Either you vote for us on Thursday or all rights for trees will be rescinded. The *Tree's Charter* will be so much *pulp*,' it added hatefully. 'What is the point of making a lone stand? Never mind your principles, think of your comrades in woods and on downlands. Millions will die. We have numberless motorway schemes waiting to be implemented. The combine-harvester lobby will take care of the hedgerows. Your cause is doomed. Vote for us.'

Giblets, no mean activist himself, felt his intestines contract as he realized that he was actually in the presence of a parliamentary candidate. He gazed at the shifty eyes, the mouth puckered from years of kissing the defenceless. How could the silver birch hope to prevail against such unalloyed evil?

The birch remained aloof, towering magisterially over the wretch who slavered at its foot. Its leaves trembled a little but it stood its ground.

Giblets, knowing that in the open air most politicians could register Force 15 on the Auger scale, was humbled by the fortitude of the young tree which betrayed its torment only by the involuntary motion of its leaves and a barely discernible tremor in its trunk. But then, of course, he told himself; it isn't being bored. It is terrified. How many other of our leafy brethren are being subjected to this extortion?

His unspoken question was answered almost immediately for the politician, with a final sneer, turned his attentions from the silver birch, leaned over the wall and gripped Hilary's lowest branch with his hand. Giblets gazed in fascinated horror at that hand, misshapen, grotesquely enlarged from years of pressing flesh.

'Little tree, little tree,' the monster crooned in malign cadences, 'will you too opt for a premature martyr's death, or will you throw in your lot with the party that truly has the interests of trees at heart, the party that *cares*, the party that takes for its patron St Hugh the Bleeder of Bruges who preached to trees.'

Giblets, still leaning against Hilary's trunk, felt a convulsion of pure horror wrench her very roots. With a little sigh the young tree made a supreme effort and tore those roots from the soil that nurtured them, at the same time twisting her branch free from the political mauler that encircled it. For an instant she teetered, lurched, whispered a leafy farewell and fell prostrate upon the earth and upon Ernest Giblets KGB, CIA, MI6 who, compressed by the combined weight of Hilary and the step-ladder, lay lifeless beneath the lifeless tree he had sought to save.

He was too late to circulate the unimaginable truth among the gardeners of Stalemate, that the Blighters, having failed to win the support of mature trees at the last election, had concentrated on trying to subvert the tender and impressionable saplings instead. But his last conscious thought was one of great pride in the knowledge that, rather than surrender to the blandishments of propagandists, these virgin martyrs had died by their own hands.

On the following Thursday morning, when the polling stations flung wide their doors and canvassers ablaze with rosettes thronged the streets, many houses in Stalemate presented curtained windows to the world, houses in whose gardens lay the blameless corpses of saplings and young trees. It was a second massacre of the innocents. Great oaks and elms and willows gazed down upon the devastation and cried aloud into the wind. The will to live had left them. Within a year not a tree was left standing in Stalemate and all through the autumn the air was made hideous by the triumphant shrieks of chainsaws as the victorious Blighters roved among the fallen and placed advertisements in the local press offering sawn logs at £25 per tipper load. It was, they said, part of their campaign to encourage local authorities to recycle waste.

As soon as the winter rains had washed away the last of the sawdust the Blighters began to appoint their own party hacks to fill the vacancies left by the trees. In every garden appeared dwarf conifers, flowering cherries, Japanese maples and buddleias; anything, in fact, that could be relied upon not to grow to more than twenty feet. These miserable pawns were indoctrinated to report any political irregularities to their masters in Whitehall, the information being fed to them by hangers-on like clematis, Virginia creepers and Russian vines. In vain did the followers of Giblets attempt to combat them with Opposition propaganda calculated to Force 3 on the Auger scale. The new trees had all been innoculated against the Glanders Effect by renegade scientists. The triumph of the Blighters was complete.

'Except in Old Compton,' I said.

'I'm beginning to wonder about Old Compton,' Elaine said.

We were up in her attic, on the tea-chest divan, leaning out of the window to stare along the length of wilderness gardens that lay behind the houses of Old Compton Street. In either direction it was leaves, as far as we could see.

'But it's all trees,' I said.

'Did you ever stop to read the *Tree's Charter*?'

Elaine said, gloomily. 'Remember how they were promised special parks, unlimited hedgerows, forestation schemes? It made no difference, they were all cut down anyway.'

'But these trees aren't going to be cut down.'

'What do you think is going to happen to this place?' Elaine said.

'This house?'

'This whole street. There's only a couple of dozen people living along here, now, and we're four of them. I think you may have got it wrong with your Creation theory. Compton Rosehay is still growing. We could only get a nine-month lease. All the land's being sold.'

I knew she was right. Those FOR SALE boards I had noticed when I first walked along the street all had SOLD stickers on them. And soon this house would be SOLD too, and Elaine would be gone.

Then the triumph of the Blighters would be complete.

—11—
There Goes the
Neighbourhood

Little had been heard of the Martians recently. People had soon forgotten where they came from. They found jobs, raised families, rented houses and then became owner-occupiers. Gradually assimilated into the community they became anxious to appear like everyone else, and in most respects they were like everyone else. They adopted a form of dress with very wide sleeves and took care never to allow more than one pair of hands to show in public for fear of being accused of having an unfair advantage when it came to playing cards, carrying shopping or applying for Housing Benefit. Rude children and men in pubs told jokes about people who could count to twenty without taking off their shoes and made snide remarks about persons with two wristwatches or more armpits than they'd had hot dinners, but on the whole, the Martians were accepted.

'Some of my best friends are Martians,' was a remark often overheard.

However, there was a small sect who went round defiantly in short sleeves, waving their arms about or ostentatiously doing something different with all four hands. They performed fiendishly complicated gymnastics and square dancing took on a whole new meaning; it became known as cube dancing. The assimilated Martians were seriously embarrassed by these 'Armigers' as they called themselves. They, after all, bent over backwards to be good neighbours with the terrestrials, joining residents' associations, lending each other step-ladders and cross-head screw-drivers and, mostly, people in Stalemate were inclined to live and let live. But the Martians had not reckoned with Zoot Humus. Zoot, of course, had stalled over the case of the Illuminated Turbot.

It was blatantly obvious, after the autopsy, that the blunt instrument that had stove in the head of the Anti-Poet was the turbot itself. Fish scales from the turbot were embedded in the Anti-Poet. Hairs from the Anti-Poet were discovered adhering to the turbot. Both turbot and Anti-Poet were found lying in the street outside the premises of Dagobert the fishmonger poet, sole source of fish, poetry and tattoos in the whole of Stalemate.

This was deeply dissatisfying to Zoot Humus. The wind had changed, whetting his appetite for duplicity. What credit would there be to him in discovering the identity of the murderer when absolutely anyone else could have deduced it from the available evidence?

Silently Zoot Humus paced the moonlit streets of Stalemate, cogitating, and in every house hearts lurched with fear and foreboding. Three weeks had passed since the turbot incident and still Dagobert had not been charged with the crime. (Dagobert, incidentally, had not confessed since he did not regard the death of an Anti-Poet as a crime. Nor did many people, but this was beside the point.) As the bat-like shadow of Humus fell across their thresholds people looked uneasily at one another—all except the Martians. Peaceable, devout and numbingly respectable, the Martians retired early to bed and slept with easy consciences, except for the Armigers. Young, arrogant and fearless, they forgathered on street corners and danced to the music of small loud stereo systems, linking their four arms in complex manoeuvres.

Hideous thoughts began to writhe through the brain of Humus. What he really hated about Stalemate was its tolerance. Since the Nuns' Riot of '76 there had not been a single case of civil unrest unless you counted the forcible isolation of Auger; or Professor Scrapie's ongoing legal proceedings against the Throat family; or the last eight general elections. The worst that Stalemate citizens seemed to be able to do was irritate, bore or blackmail the neighbours. What Zoot Humus yearned to do was to set them all at each other's throats in a cataclysm of rage, greed, resentment, envy and fear. So far he had achieved only fear and that very much on a one-to-one basis. How could he ensure that everyone suffered?

'Divide and rule?' said the conscience of Zoot Humus, a wasted, vestigial organ that accidentally had been almost completely removed along with his tonsils when he was young, and now malfunctioned, coming up with the most degenerate suggestions.

'I want everyone to suffer equally,' Zoot replied.

'Can't be done,' said the conscience, 'but you can certainly make them suffer unequally. You can generate rage, greed, envy and resentment in the majority. All you need for that is a minority. They will supply the fear.'

And one word came unbidden to his lips: *Martians.*

If Dagobert had had any kind of a conscience, no matter how vestigial, he would have been deeply suspicious or even alarmed when, answering his entry-phone one evening, he heard the voice of Zoot Humus requesting fish. However, all he said was, 'You know what to do,' and went to the window to watch his customer cross the road.

> 'Bliss was it in that dawn to be alive,
> But to be a TURBOT was very heaven,'

sang Humus, in the gloaming, but Dagobert's heart skipped never a beat. He merely felt slightly annoyed that for once he would be unable to supply the item demanded.

'Fresh out of turbot,' he said, as Zoot Humus came up the stairs. 'I had one a few weeks back but somebody must have bought it. That is, somebody must have bought my sestina entitled "Up to the hips in a mountain stream with a rod and a line and a fly" which was tattooed upon it. I wouldn't have let a sestina go to someone who just wanted fish.'

'Is it possible then to obtain fish from these premises *without* the poetry?' inquired Humus.

'Of course it is,' Dagobert said, percussing on a pouting where he was practising hexameters. 'If you wanted poetry you would not have been singing the fish song, you would have been composing a haiku in three minutes flat on the subject of monkfish.'

'Then how come Professor Scrapie had a triolet on his salmon which was, so my investigations have revealed, eaten by, among others, the gentleman who was struck down dead on your doorstep only three weeks ago?'

'Scrapie must have been misinformed,' Dagobert said. 'He came to me for a triolet which I then, at his request, tattooed on a salmon. If he subsequently ate the salmon, that's his affair. Possibly he had first memorized the triolet. He could have saved me a lot of time and himself a lot of money if he had just asked for the salmon.'

'Poetry's dearer than fish, then, is it?' Humus said.

'Man hours,' Dagobert replied. Humus was thinking, This person exhibits no sign of fear, remorse or even dishonesty. There is certainly no point in charging him with the murder. He hasn't lost a second's sleep over it. He appears to have forgotten that he committed it. I shall put my plan into action.

'Well, anyhow,' Humus said. 'I made a mistake.

Now that I'm here, I suppose you would not object to providing me with a fish as requested.'

'I told you, I have no turbot.'

'I don't actually want a turbot.'

'I heard you, distinctly, singing my fish song on the other side of the road. "To be a turbot was very heaven", you sang.'

'I simply wished to gain access. I want a poem. I want a poem on a fish. Turbot happened to come to mind, but squid would do.'

'I've got a squid in the freezer,' Dagobert said.

'Already tattooed?'

'A limerick. I was just trifling.'

'That won't do,' Humus said. 'I need a poem, never mind the metre, never mind the length; written to order.'

'On what subject?'

'On the joy of having four arms,' Humus said.

'I have only two arms,' said Dagobert. 'I like it that way. It would compromise my integrity to pretend otherwise. Personally I should think that having four arms is a bloody nuisance.'

'Good grief,' said Humus, 'you can compose a poem without *meaning* it, can't you?'

'I advise you to leave before I kick you downstairs,' said Dagobert. 'If you want fiction go and look for a novelist.'

'A few lines is all I ask,' Humus said. He was nonplussed. He had never before encountered anyone so unimpressionable as Dagobert. He was impossible to threaten, menace or terrorize. He was an artist. But, and here the heart of Humus lightened, unlike many artists he had, as it were, more than one string to his bow.

'Hang about,' Humus said, 'when people come to you for a tattoo, they don't always ask for one of your poems, do they?'

'Very rarely,' said Dagobert, frankly. 'Look here, first you want fish, then you want poetry, now you're talking about tattoos. Make up your mind.'

'All right,' said Humus, 'I want a tattoo. If I asked you to tattoo *Zoot loves Lucy* on my biceps, would you do it?'

'Of course,' Dagobert said. 'I should prefer not to, but I wouldn't refuse.'

'Is there *anything* that you would refuse to tattoo on me?'

'Nothing—unless of an obscene or defamatory nature. And nothing political, no *Martians go home* or anything like that.'

'Quite the reverse,' said Humus, wondering if there was anything in telepathy at all. How gratifying to be able to scare people to death without going anywhere near them. 'Now, listen, I want a tattoo, but I do not want it on me. I want it on a fish. I want you to tattoo a fish with complimentary things about Martians, especially about how wonderful it is to have four arms. You can enclose it in a heart, surround it with bluebirds and roses, but it must be on a fish. Do I make myself clear?'

'Adequately,' said Dagobert. 'All right. I'll do you six lines on a flounder. Come back tomorrow. Beat on the door in five-four time.'

Next afternoon Humus took delivery of his flounder, wrapped in newspaper, and hurried home to see what he had got for his money. At first sight he wondered if he had perhaps overestimated Dagobert's genius. On the flounder was inscribed:

> *Hooray!* *I love being a Martian,*
> *I love having four arms.*
> *Yippee!* *I love having four elbows,*
> *No matter how hard the gale blows.*

Wow!   I love having four wrists.
I love having four fists.

On the other hand, he had to admit, there was no
mistaking its sentiments. He put the flounder in his
refrigerator, after first carefully scraping off several
scales with a spatula. Then he went along to The
Mugger's Arms where at that hour of the day he
could be sure of finding Lord Tod.

His lordship was, as usual, ensconced in a shadowy
corner looking uneasily out of the tail of his eye at
the bartender, Gregory McCadaver, who was picking out the *Hallelujah Chorus* on his front teeth.

'He used to be at The Cod's Head,' Tod complained when he saw Zoot Humus bearing down
upon him. 'I started coming here to get away from
him. I suspect that he is in the pay of the lawyer
Jones, keeping an eye on me.'

'Why ever should he be doing that?' asked Humus,
who knew perfectly well why, since he too was a
member of the Stalemate Blackmail Co-operative.
Without waiting for an answer he went on, 'I won't
beat about the bush, Tod. I need a corpse.'

'Why come to me?' Tod asked, blenching.

'If I can refrain from beating about the bush, so
can you,' said Humus. 'And anyway, there's no need
to look so terrified.' He was aware that Tod would
have been terrified if Humus had asked him for a
light as, indeed, would anyone in Stalemate, except
Dagobert.

'I thought you already had a corpse,' said Tod. 'I
understood you already had a corpse—and a fish.'
Little ripples of fear spread over the surface of his
Polish vodka.

'Wrong corpse, wrong fish,' said Humus. 'Now,
be a good wretch and let me have a body. In
exchange, I'll let you have mine.'

'The one you're wearing?' Tod said, hopefully.

'Don't be ridiculous,' Humus said, 'I'm talking about the one you rashly mentioned in connection with a fish.'

'I suppose you want to come and choose it—look, let's get out of here,' Tod said, noticing that Gregory McCadaver was ten bars into Ravel's *Bolero* which had been known to register force 8 on the Auger scale even when played by the Berlin Philharmonic.

They strolled together through the midday streets of Stalemate and Tod could not help noticing that although the sun was almost over his head and his shadow was almost underneath his feet, the shadow of Zoot Humus stretched long and menacing in all directions; all whom it touched shrank away and, depending upon their religion, made signs to neutralize its evil influence. All except the Martians, who might have wanted to make signs but were too much concerned with keeping their hands out of sight.

When they reached Lord Tod's demesne the shadow of Humus was absorbed into all the other shadows that spread themselves about the leafy glades and alleys of the Manor Garth.

'I don't want anything very *long*,' Humus said, thinking to himself, Martians are shortish people. Dagobert's victim was at least as tall as I. No Martian could have struck him down with a flounder. 'Nothing above five feet six, if you please.'

'It's no good looking in there,' Tod said, seeing Humus trying the door of a small potting shed. 'That's just what's left over when Gleet has had his pick—for the mermaid factory. I imagine you want a head on yours.'

'Certainly I want a head,' Humus said. 'The head is the most important part. I mean to say, you can hardly have cranial injuries without a head, can you?'

Tod conducted his visitor into the manor itself,

down a flight of steps to the cellar. 'I'll leave you to choose,' he said.

Humus looked all around, at the shelves. 'Mummies, by Jove,' he said.

'You didn't expect fresh ones?' Tod demanded.

'They aren't all yours, surely?'

'What do you take me for?' said Tod. 'My predecess—my relative, the late Lord Tod, laid the foundations of the collection. I just add to it here and there.'

'You needn't lie to me,' said Humus. 'Don't forget that I *know*.'

'Know what?'

'That ever since you inherited the title you have been frantically accumulating loose corpses in case one of them turns out to be the lost claimant.'

'I just like collecting the dead,' Tod murmured carelessly.

'Have you added anyone lately?' Humus asked eagerly. 'Anyone you haven't er . . . processed?'

'We had a consignment of Throats not long ago,' said Tod, 'but they're salting down nicely. There's one upstairs that I haven't begun work on.'

Humus followed his host back up the steps to the laboratory. 'You'll have to be quick,' Tod said. 'Gleet's got his eye on this one.'

'It'll do,' Humus cried, whipping out his tape measure. 'Now, I want you to observe my next actions very carefully since you will, in due course, be called as a material witness.'

From his pocket he withdrew a spatula and scraped it ostentatiously across the head of the corpse. 'Look at that!' he cried in triumph, holding out the spatula for Tod's inspection, at the same time interposing a magnifying glass. 'What do you see?'

'Fish scales,' said Tod.

'Flounder scales, to be precise,' said Humus, at the

same time helping himself to a strand or two of hair. 'This is the body which was found lying lifeless at the foot of the steps outside the premises of Dagobert the poet,' he added, scrupulously omitting any reference to Dagobert's other activities.

'You could have fooled me,' said Tod. 'I understood it to be a certain – '

'You were misinformed,' Humus said. 'This is the body in question, stuck down by a flounder.'

'I'd heard it was a turbot.'

'Wrong again. It was a flounder. I have the said flounder in my refrigerator at this very moment. When I have proved that the scales match, I shall arrest the culprit.'

'You mean, you know who owns the flounder?'

'Taking into consideration certain distinguishing marks,' said Humus, 'I can prove that the flounder could only have been the property of one or several of a certain group of people.'

'Distinguishing marks?' Tod said. 'Fingerprints?'

'Among others,' Humus said. 'But, even more precisely, written proof that the owner had, ho, ho, more armpits than he'd had hot dinners. Say no more. D'you follow me?'

'I can hardly believe it,' Tod said, knowing that in fact he was not required to believe it, only to repeat it which, being anxious to stay in Zoot's good books, he immediately did, in The Cod's Head, The Mugger's Arms and The Frog's Legs.

Humus meanwhile went home, took his evidence out of the fridge and walked purposefully back to the centre of Stalemate, pleasantly aware that already rumours were circulating nervously and that people were according him their usual looks of fear and loathing disguised as abject adoration. A whole bouquet of orchids was tossed at him as he passed God's.

The Martians lived mainly in the area of Restharrow and Goat's Lea. No one would have dreamed of calling it a ghetto, nevertheless there were a lot of Martians about, which suited Zoot's plan perfectly. Crossing the road he appeared to trip, he appeared to fling out an arm to save himself, the flounder appeared to fly out of his hands. What certainly did happen, however, was that a public-spirited Martian leapt forward and caught the flounder as it began its downward arc and saved it from falling into the dust; planting on it, quite incidentally, four perfect sets of fingerprints.

'Yours, I think,' said the Martian as Humus appeared to recover his balance.

'Why, surely not,' said Zoot.

'But you were carrying it,' the Martian said.

'Oh, indeed, it was in my possession,' said Humus. 'It was and it is. It is evidence. This is the fish that caused the death of a man three weeks ago . . . you may remember the circumstances.'

'I do,' said the Martian. 'I remember that the murder weapon was said to be a turbot.'

'That was before I began my investigations,' Humus said. 'I have now proved conclusively that this flounder was the murder weapon. Scales brushed from its body were found upon the dead man's person. Hairs from the dead man were found upon the flounder. My goodness, look. There's something written on it.'

The Martian quickly scanned Dagobert's six lines on the pleasures of owning four arms. 'That's nice,' he said, innocently.

'Can you imagine anyone who didn't have four arms finding any aesthetic or technical merit at all in that doggerel?' Humus demanded.

'It does rhyme,' the Martian said, defensively.

'And of course,' said Humus, 'unless the original criminal wore gloves, *this flounder will bear his finger-*

prints. I shall return,' said Humus, and walked away, leaving the Martian wringing all his hands and watched by curious passers-by who had unaccountably failed to witness the incident.

By tea-time the word had passed around Stalemate that Zoot Humus was about to unmask the murderer. Zoot, and the flounder, were in The Mugger's Arms as usual, and a magnifying glass lay to hand upon the bar, should anyone request to examine the four sets of fingerprints more closely. But no one felt the need to examine anything closely. Instead they were gathering in large numbers outside the houses of Martians, shouting, chanting and throwing things. Martians were jostled in shops and attacked on buses, their coat sleeves were ripped off and Martian jokes were shouted in a threatening manner.

A number of patriotic citizens, unwilling to be accused of mindless vandalism, called a meeting outside the town hall and organized themselves into orderly platoons armed with bricks and pickaxe handles, many still with the pickaxe heads attached. Then they dispersed, still in good order, along Restharrow and Goat's Lea, patriotically breaking windows and looting shops that were known to be owned by Martians. The contents were removed quite systematically; the proceedings could in no way be described as mindless.

As darkness fell less disciplined elements of the population converted concrete fencing posts into battering rams and commenced smashing their way into Martian houses, hurling chairs and television sets out of the windows and driving the occupants, who were mainly sheltering in upstairs rooms, into the street. Vehicles in adjoining garages mysteriously caught alight and clouds of oily smoke, flickering redly within, like thunderheads, obscured the stars. At ten-thirty the Martian temple went up in flames.

'Do you think the services of the Stalemate Black-mail Co-operative will be required?' asked the lawyer Jones, when he joined Zoot in the saloon bar just before closing time.

'I doubt if there will be anyone left to blackmail by morning,' Zoot replied, sunnily. He slung his opera cloak negligently over his shoulder, donned his fedora at a debonair angle and strolled out of The Mugger's Arms. His prediction about the blackmail was correct. When the sun rose it shone upon the empty houses of Goat's Lea and Restharrow. Some-how, during the hours of darkness, the Martians had left Stalemate, on a night of violence and turmoil. It was summer . . .

We did not know quite what to make of the Martian episode; it seemed to have acquired its own momen-tum, out of our control.

All Elaine said afterwards was, 'Clearly one of those occasions when Earth's fabric wore completely threadbare.'

It struck me that it was one of those increasingly frequent occasions when Stalemate seemed more real than Compton Rosehay.

—12—
Widdershins

The first exam was English Language and it was scheduled for next morning. Elaine and I decided that if you didn't know your own language by the age of sixteen, sitting up all night to revise would be little help, so we *said* we were going to revise—we even said it to each other—and went to sit in the churchyard of what had once, long ago, been Rosehay.

'We could practise our verbs,' I said. 'Conjugate the verb "to sit".'

'I sit, you sit, hesheorit sits, we sit, you sit, they sit. I wonder why English is supposed to be so difficult for foreigners to learn.'

'It can't be that difficult,' I said. 'They all seem to learn it. I think it must be the spelling.'

'S—I—T, yes. Hellish.'

'And the sound. Think of goes and does. They look the same. If you didn't know, you'd think they were goze and doze or guz and duz.'

We had been sitting in the churchyard for half an hour, and nothing had happened. Usually we had to be together only for about two minutes before a Stalemate story began to unfold. I had suggested the churchyard because I had been sure that there we would learn the hitherto suppressed facts about the McCadavers or Lord Tod's mummification programme. We never had got very far with investigating the McCadavers. Their main attribute appeared to be that there were a lot of them but apart from Nigel they never seemed to get more than a walking-on part, answering the door, serving in a pub or working at the library. I had a theory that McCadav-

ers only ever married other McCadavers and that
centuries of inbreeding had produced a family who
were all eerily identical, with some shared distinguishing feature, both eyes on the same side of the
head, perhaps, like flatfish. Maybe there had been
a wicked 19th century Squire McCadaver who had
stridden about in riding boots, twirling his whiskers
and seducing Stalemate maidens who might then
marry their regular sweethearts in haste, but when
the by-blows were born, there was the dread mark
of the McCadavers for all to see.

Had there been a 19th century in Stalemate? Well,
it would have been some time before '76, anyway.

'The Curse of the McCadavers . . .' I said, exper-
imentally, but Elaine did not respond. She stood up
from the bench where we were sitting and began to
walk slowly along the row of gravestones that ran
from the bench beside the path to the south porch of
the church. It was a dull little churchyard, no yews
or willows, no urns or angels, no vaults or crypts or
table tombs, no mausoleums; unlike the cemetery
where Aneesa and I used to spend hours, doing our
homework and talking about sex in case some ever
came our way. Sometimes we'd hang on till dusk
began to fall, on winter afternoons, just to frighten
ourselves.

It was difficult to imagine that the dead of Rosehay
walked by night; if they walked at all they probably
got up at 7 a.m. like everyone else, and put in office
hours. The church was still in use, but that was
empty of everything except pews and a sad Sunday
School corner with pictures of saints stuck to the wall
about one metre from the floor, and a horseshoe of
very tiny chairs. Soon, we suspected, the church
would be sold as a site of great potential with planning permission and the tombstones would be lev-
elled so that the churchyard could be landscaped. It

seemed to me that Rosehay had never had a chance, and with Elaine's talk about expansion and development I began to fear that Old Compton would meet the same fate, and if Old Compton went, how should we be able to find the way into Stalemate?

Elaine was walking back towards me, tapping the top of each gravestone as she passed it as if she were counting to see if they added up to the same number coming and going.

'What's happening to the Plantagenets?' I said, a shade desperately. What was the matter? Stalemate was waiting for us, why couldn't we go in and walk its horrid streets? 'Has anyone seen Richard III lately?'

'You know, if you walk widdershins round a church, you disappear,' Elaine said.

'Widdershins?'

'Anti-clockwise.'

'What's clockwise, then?'

'Deasil. Come on, let's walk widdershins and see what happens. I've got something to tell you.'

I'd been afraid of that. I got up from the bench and we set off, keeping very close to the churchyard wall, so that we would have farther to walk, heading east, north, west, south; widdershins.

'We're moving,' Elaine said, at last, when we reached the south-east corner and turned left. 'We're moving soon.'

We were half-way along the east side, directly opposite the end of the church, before I could say, 'When?'

'As soon as the exams are over. We could go at the end of this month, but Marge and John didn't want to disrupt my studies—no, they didn't actually *say* that, but that's what they meant.'

'I didn't think you'd be going so soon.' We had arrived at the north-east corner, and turned again.

'All that work your dad's been doing on the house . . .'

'There was woodworm. He couldn't leave it in case it spread to our stuff. I told you it was only a nine months' let. We'd have had to go in August, anyway.'

'Where are you going?'

'Derbyshire. A viaduct. You remember we were hoping for a suspension bridge. This is the next best thing, better in a way. It's already there.'

The north side of the churchyard was flanked by a row of maisonettes, St Margaret's Walk. Perhaps McCadavers lived there. I kept thinking of those wasted months before we had discovered Stalemate, when Elaine had just been someone who sat at the table where people who didn't matter sat. She had been there for five months, not mattering, while I hung around with Rowena and Marie and Lynzi, talking about cellulite and diets and *Macbeth* and Peter Rafferty who had just been done for possession.

'I did say we'd be moving.'

'Yes, but so soon . . .' Moving what? Paul's tent, the tea-chests that Elaine had never unpacked, the matting runner in the hall that curled up at the end, I had learned, not because people kept tripping over it but because it never got the chance to relax after being rolled up, rather like Elaine's mother. 'What about the carrots?' Poor Marge Crossley, doomed yet again to leave her crop unharvested.

'You promised to eat them for us.'

My mind leapt ahead to the summer holidays, me in the garden of the abandoned house, knee high in grass and weeds, fossicking for the carrots and eating them in pious remembrance of the Crossleys, choking on every mouthful.

At the north-west corner of the churchyard was a compost heap. Very few of the graves had fresh flowers so the compost heap was low and dry, topped up with nothing more exciting than grass clippings. In Stoke Newington, Aneesa and I used to plunder the heaps for flowers that were still quite fresh and smuggle out bouquets under our coats.

'We can ring each other, write; you can come and stay,' Elaine said as we walked, more slowly all the time, along the western side of the churchyard. The wall was low. You could see the roof of Glanders quite clearly from there, rearing up above the other houses.

'Where are you going to live?'

'It's another new town, Halesforth. But it's a real new town. John brought a brochure home. I mean, it's not *that* new, it was built in the 1960s, but it *looks* as if it was built in the 1960s. You can see that it's meant to be modern.'

'God didn't create it, then?'

'Shouldn't think he's been near the place.'

I was thinking, What's going to happen next term? Marie's leaving but Rowena and Lynzi'll still be there. And I shan't have Elaine. What have I done? I shan't have anyone. They won't just sneer at me, they'll be sorry for me. Not properly sorry, pitying. Rowena called Elaine my lezzie friend, they'll never let up. I felt as though I'd been away somewhere, for a long time, and had been sent home in disgrace, and everyone knew about it.

I wailed, 'I can't do Stalemate on my own.'

'Is there anything left?' Elaine said. 'We've killed off just about everyone in it.'

That hadn't struck me before, but when I looked back I saw the trail of destruction we'd left in our wake; the repatriated Martians, the decimated Throats, hundreds of expunged nuns, Auger lique- fied by his own boredom, Dagobert in the freezer, not to mention the mummified results of Lord Tod's little hobby. Somehow, at the time, we hadn't noticed.

'Do you think that's significant?' I said. We had reached the final, south-west corner.

'We have to be careful from now on,' Elaine said. 'In a minute we'll be back where we started. If we're going to disappear, this is where it happens.'

'Why?'

'Well, it hasn't happened yet. Is what significant?'

'That as fast as we discovered people we finished them off.'

'It either says a lot about Stalemate or a lot about us. I suppose the McCadavers will go from strength to strength. The Plantagenets have been around for hundreds of years. Sooner or later Richard III will come into his own.'

'We never even found out where they lived.'

We were almost back at the bench where we had been sitting. I willed us to keep walking, to keep talking, for Elaine to reveal that all along the Plantagenets had been holed up in a house in Sennacre or Osier Bank, or even down the road from us in Coldharbour, but when we got to the bench we sat down again.

'Well, we didn't disappear,' Elaine said.

'How do you know? We can't tell if we've disappeared until we meet someone and say hello and they don't see us.'

'I don't think it happens like that,' Elaine said. 'I think we'd actually *be* somewhere else.'

'We've been somewhere else for weeks.'

'And now we've come back.'

'You'll miss Hallowe'en in Stalemate, when the young men dress up with wreaths of scurfwort in their hair and rush around the town at midnight boyishly pouring paraffin through people's letter boxes.'

'And St Hugh's Day, when the sacred sword of St Hugh the Bleeder is garlanded with stockbroker's nightshade and paraded through the streets.'

'And Christmas, when the schoolchildren gather on street corners with half bricks and threaten to sing unless people give them money.' It was no good. I couldn't keep it up. 'What am I going to do?' I said.

'What about me?'

'You'll have escaped. I'll still be here.'

'So will Stalemate. Remember, Earth's fabric hath worn thin. Our mistake has been thinking that we were making Stalemate up. We weren't. We only discovered it. It wasn't a game, it was real. It still is. It's all happening. It doesn't need us.'

No, it didn't need us, but we needed it, or rather, *I* needed it, much more, I saw now, than Elaine had ever done. 'You know what's happened, don't you?' I said, bitterly. 'Sodding widdershins! *We* haven't disappeared—Stalemate has.'

It was true. We had never talked *about* Stalemate before, not since the day we first discovered it. Somewhere, as we walked widdershins round Rosehay church, we had lost it.

The Crossleys moved out on July 11th. The only remotely cheerful thing that happened at that time was that at some moment, under her red king-size duvet cover, Mrs Cattermole became pregnant again, which meant that for nine months the Big Knickers would be getting bigger, along with her, and at the end of that time there would be a second generation of nappies invading our privacy when the wind was in the west.

It was almost the end of the summer holidays before I could bring myself to revisit the house in Old Compton, the last weekend in August, when I had received two important pieces of news. One was my GCSE results and I had passed everything; I had even passed some things with Grade As, and my parents were so pleased. Over the last few months I had hardly noticed them, except as voices in the background.

'We didn't like to say anything,' Mum confided, after we'd done a bit of modest celebrating at Robin Hood's, 'but you seemed so worried, off on your own all the time. But you must have been working so hard. We *are* proud of you.'

I actually felt bad about that. Of course I hadn't been off on my own, worrying and studying in secret, I had been in Stalemate with Elaine. But then, they never knew about Elaine. The nearest my mother had ever come to knowing was that one time when she had left a message on the television screen, from Eileen. And I hadn't been working hard at all. Perhaps I was cleverer than I thought.

From the doorway of Robin Hood's I could look across the pedestrian precinct to Jangles Coffee House. Rowena had just gone in with her parents; she too had something to celebrate. We had even congratulated each other that morning, when we all went to pick up the results. We were speaking again. I looked in at Jangles window as I walked with Mum and Dad to the car park, to wave to Rowena. Perhaps the yoghurt maker's rep had complained, because the sign had been moved out from behind the espresso machine. You could see it all, now: *Frozen yoghurt*.

The other piece of news was a letter from Elaine, in answer to one I'd written her—no, we weren't ringing each other. She'd written it before her results came though, but she'd probably got straight As. It wasn't a very interesting letter; all about Halesforth, and the new house, which was a real new house, not just new to the Crossleys for once, and they were going to stay in it. John and Marge had had enough of uprooting themselves and were going to settle. I thought that it was a pity that they hadn't decided to settle a bit sooner instead of uprooting Paul and Elaine every year or so, but, I remembered, they had done it so that they could all stay together, and if they had settled sooner it wouldn't have been in Compton Rosehay, and I would never have met Elaine.

Soon it would be the turn of Paul and Elaine themselves to uproot for ever.

She did not mention Stalemate once, but then, in my letter, neither had I, except for a tentative, almost obligatory, comment about the Plantagenets. The nearest Elaine came to mentioning any of the past we had shared was in the postscript, written up the side of the paper, for lack of space. *Marge sends her love and says don't forget the carrots.*

I had forgotten the carrots, but after the letter I went down to Old Compton. Not straight down, it took me two or three days to pluck up not so much the courage as the will to go back. I went the way I had first gone, past the school, round the back of the sports hall and down the alley. The thorn branches overhead were red with haws and the fruit trees in the forgotten gardens were heavy with apples and plums that had been frothy with blossom that first afternoon. On the wasteland, willowherb had grown two metres tall and seeded, but the cards in the Post Office were still there, still advertising the green lady's bycicle and the ginger kitten. I walked along to Elaine's house, pushed open the gate in the overgrown privet and walked through the long grass — I'd been right about that — to the strip of cultivated garden where Marge Crossley had planted her carrots as a kind of votive offering: Please God, let me stay here long enough to see them grow.

The vegetable plot was almost as overgrown as the rest of the garden, but among the grasses and docks and evening primroses, the ferny heads of the carrots could be seen. Starting at one end of the row I worked my way along, carefully tugging and twisting. It was a bumper crop. The carrots were perfect, long, straight and vibrantly orange and when I held the whole bunch in my arms the ferns fell back like green trailing hair. For a moment I almost thought of mermaids.

I had brought a carrier bag for the carrots. I packed them in and stood for a little while longer in the garden, looking up at the attic window where Elaine and I had sat so often on the divan made from two tea-chests with a rug thrown across them. I peered in through the dusty window at the empty kitchen, hoping that something of the Crossleys remained, but there was nothing there, not even dead flies. From the washing line hung a dishcloth, grey, stiff and lean, the only thing they had left behind.

Dark clouds were threatening. I thought I would go on to the end of Old Compton Street and catch the bus home, so I left the garden without looking at the front door which had once stood always open and was now shut for ever, and set out to walk to the bus stop.

On the far side of the road stood *The Old Forge Antiques*. I don't think either of us had looked in at its window since the day we met there and the Martians landed. I crossed over to see if anything had been sold since March. The leather-bound bible was still on display, along with two of the chamber pots, but the footstool and the third chamber pot had gone. Where the wash basin and jug had stood there was now a green and yellow pottery jardinière with a spiny plant growing in it. Right at the front of the window was the alabaster thing with the brass thing stuck in it. The Old Forge was open. I went in.

The proprietor was not old and pathetic and

defeated, she couldn't have been more than thirty, and I knew her. I'd seen her in lycra, turning up at school for aerobics. She recognized me too, I could tell, by the way she seemed surprised to see me. What she didn't seem surprised about was having a customer.

'That thing in the window,' I said, 'that thing at the front . . .'

I'd meant to say, 'How much is it?' as a way of setting things going, but instead I said, 'What is it?'

Mrs Old Forge moved a pleated silk screen and reached into the window.

'It's a pen stand,' she said, handing it to me. I could see that now, I'd always thought it must be something like that. There was a groove cut along the front of the alabaster block. 'There was probably an ink pot or something like that to go with it. You know what it's made from, don't you?'

That was what I had gone in to find out, but I almost said, 'Don't tell me.'

'It's a horse brass,' she said. 'Rather an unusual one. I imagine it must have been fixed on the bridle, between the ears. It would have jingled beautifully.'

She shook the thing slightly. Did I, for a second, hear the clink of Nightgown's holy medals?

'It's fifteen pounds,' said Mrs Old Forge. 'The alabaster's not worth much but the horse brass is quite rare. You so seldom see a real one these days.'

'Thanks, but I can't afford it,' I said, which was true, but I also knew that I didn't want it. Mrs Old Forge didn't seem to mind; she must have been used to people not being able to afford things. I had just noticed the price tag on one of the chamber pots and I had also noticed that the back of the shop was full of really beautiful furniture. The Old Forge was not the sorrowful relic I had imagined. People probably came from miles around to buy antiques there.

I left the shop and saw a hand putting the Martian's holy relic back in the window. I went up to the top of the concrete road, past Gleeson's garage where the mechanics were wheeling out a suspiciously shiny Peugeot, and caught the bus back through the Manor Garth to Coldharbour. I'd been wondering what to do with the carrots—I couldn't eat them all—but when I got in, my mother swooped on them.

'Oh, what beauties,' she said. 'Where did you get those?'

'Friend's garden,' I said. 'I'll just take one to eat now.'

My mother was looking wistfully at the carrots, and stroking the ferns as if they were alive and would purr. 'I haven't seen any like that for years,' she said. 'Have you, Gwen?'

It was only then that I noticed Mrs Cattermole, swelling visibly and sitting at the kitchen table with a mug of coffee. She looked quite at home, not at all like someone who was in the middle of a row about washing lines. As I went upstairs I began to wonder guiltily if, on that morning back in the spring, Mum might not have been joking about the Big Knickers. I might have imagined the rest. After all, Mum always had made jokes, back in Stoke Newington, jokes that had Dad and me rolling around laughing. Had I thought she'd stopped making them, or had I stopped thinking that they were jokes? All the time that I'd been skulking in Stalemate with Elaine, she and Dad might have been carrying on as usual, and now that I had come home at last, there they still were, waiting for me. I wondered too if secretly I wasn't glad to be back. Compton Rosehay might be faked and phoney, but what showed through when Earth's fabric wore thin was much, much worse.

I washed the carrot in the bathroom and went to my own room to answer Elaine's letter. I meant to tell her about the GCSE results, and ask about hers, to assure Marge that the carrots had done her proud and were receiving the admiration due to them. First, though, I wanted to tell Elaine about the horse brass, but once I had started writing, it began to come out a different way.

The Martians, I wrote, *came to Stalemate on a night of luminous calm. It was summer . . .*

aidan chambers

POSTCARDS FROM NO MAN'S LAND

In a richly layered novel, spanning fifty years, Aidan Chambers powerfully evokes the atmosphere of war while brilliantly inter-weaving Jacob's exploration of new relationships in contemporary Amsterdam.

Jacob Todd, abroad on his own for the first time, arrives in Amsterdam for the commemoration of the Battle of Arnhem, where his grandfather fought fifty years before. There, Geertrui Wesseling, now a terminally ill old lady, tells an extraordinary story of love and betrayal which links Jacob with her own Dutch family in a way he never suspected and which leads him to question his place in the world.

'*A superbly crafted, intensely moving novel*' SUNDAY TELEGRAPH
'*Emotive and thought-provoking*' THE BOOKSELLER
'*...the type of serious teenage fiction that should be cherished*' THE INDEPENDENT
'*Writing and literature at its best*' SCHOOL LIBRARIAN
'*Remarkable for ... clear-eyed self-reflection that also characterises* **The Diary of Anne Frank** *and the Rembrandt portraits which Jacob so admires*' TES
'*A terrific novel*' DAILY TELEGRAPH

Winner of the 1999 Carnegie medal
Winner of the 1999 Stockport Book Award

ISBN 0099408627   £5.99